P. F.

⁎WELCOMING COMMITTEE⁎

Quinn walked over to the cage and peered into it, and O'Brien turned his head and stared into those psychotic eyes, with their mirthless, sadistic glittering. "He don't look so special to me, warden," Quinn said in a quiet, hard voice that put a chill down the backs of the prisoners.

"Well, take it from me," a deputy said, "he's as mean as they come."

Two guards went inside the cage and began dragging O'Brien out feet first. The prisoner kicked out savagely with his bound feet at the closest one and broke the man's knee cap. The other guard, in sudden panic, jumped headlong out the open cage door.

"You haven't been here a half hour, and you've caused trouble," the warden said. "Well, we got ways of handling troublemakers at Bradenville. We'll start out with solitary confinement in the hot box and work up from there."

BUFFALO HUNTER #1

HELLHOLE

Ralph Hayes

LEISURE BOOKS NEW YORK CITY

A LEISURE BOOK

Published by

Nordon Publications, Inc.
Two Park Avenue
New York, N.Y. 10016

1

The brightly painted medicine drummer's wagon straddled the small grassy knoll in the new light of a cool dawn, the garish hues of the contraption standing harsh against the soft earth colors of the surrounding plain. The lettering on the wagon announced, *Professor Ludwig's Miracle Cures*, listing such wares as nostrums, emetics, balsams and liniments, and, in smaller print, claiming the powers of accurate diagnosis by feeling the bumps on the customer's head.

The wagon sat near a stand of cottonwood, and it was surrounded by catclaw and wild pear. Beyond the trees, a creek ran swift and shallow. Near the wagon, a fire from the previous night was slowly guttering out, and a team of dun mares was staked out with short picket ropes at the trees.

As the sun cleared the horizon, an adolescent girl climbed from the wagon and moved to the fire, placing some fresh wood on it, she set a coffee pot there to boil. Her name was Charity Jenkins.

Charity was a mildly pretty girl, and was the niece and legal ward of Emil Ludwig, and a deaf-mute. She worked in the traveling medicine show for her uncle, as did her brother Uriah. The professor and Uriah were still on their hard beds in the wagon.

Charity returned to the wagon and banged on it twice with her hand, and there was a grumbling from inside which she could not hear. She smiled, knowing of the grumbling without hearing it, and reached for a towel and bar of soap on an outside shelf. She would go take a morning bath in the creek, and when she returned, the professor would be at the fire, red-eyed and bilious, mumbling some profanity at Uriah because he had arisen after the professor. Charity walked over to the trees and through them to the creek.

When she arrived there, she stood for a moment and enjoyed the morning. She was out of sight of the wagon. There was a gentle breeze off the plain, and it felt good to her as she stripped off her half boots and blouse and whipcord shirt and then her underclothing. She waded into the water and it tingled her flesh. Out in the middle, which was waist-deep, she had just begun to lather the soap in her hands when the riders appeared without warning on the crest of the far bank of the stream.

Charity, exposed from the waist upward, gasped sharply when she saw the three mounted men, and a soundless cry moved her throat. Her eyes reflected sudden fear, and when she saw the eyes on her body, her face colored and she lowered herself further into the water.

The three men sat their mounts arrogantly, grinning down at the nude girl. They were a hard-looking lot. The big heavy man in the middle made a sound in his throat. "Well, looky what you can find out on the plains if you get up early enough in the morning." His voice was hard and rasping and made something tighten inside Charity. "This ought to interest you, Ayers, you being a lady's man and all."

The unkempt, slovenly man speaking was Reuben Latimer, and it was said of him that he was more animal than human. He was a thick-shouldered man with a stubble of beard and a sweat-stained shirt. He wore the broad-rimmed blue hat and pants of a cavalry officer he had killed just before he had recently deserted from the militia, bringing the other two men with him. He was very fast with a gun, but preferred killing with his hands.

"Pretty little thing," Ayers said softly, moving his mount down to the water's edge and studying Charity with intent eyes. "Must be from the wagon we saw over there yonder."

Willis Ayers was very serious about women. He was a convicted rapist who was sought by the law in three states. When he saw a women he liked the looks of, he generally took her, and he liked what he had seen of Charity. He was a thin, lanky man with a bony face and cold eyes that seemed to stare through you. He wore a Colt on his hip, but was an expert marksman with the rifle he carried in the saddleboot.

The third man, stocky with a mustache and a lined face, was known simply as Sarge, and still wore a blue shirt with sergeant's stripes as the remnant of his army issue. He was a clever, hard man who had little patience with diversions like this that did not have the potential of turning a profit, and he was the brains behind Reuben's brief leadership of the small group.

"How can you two think of women at this time of the morning?" he said acidly.

"I always thought they looked good in the morning," Reuben answered him, moving his mount down to the water beside Ayers.

"Reckon you take them where you find them," Ayers said in that quiet voice, never taking his eyes off the frightened Charity.

Charity had let the soap slip from her grasp and float downstream, forgotten. She could not speak to them or cry out to the men at the wagon. She motioned for them to leave her, by moving her arm, but only succeeded in exposing herself again and drawing a low whistle from Ayers.

"She's a mute," Sarge told them. "See, she can't talk at all, or she'd of yelled to the wagon by now."

"That's the best kind of woman," Reuben said in his deep gravelly voice. "The ones that can't talk back."

"Go on, honey," Ayers said, grinning. "Get out of the water and get your clothes. That's what you want to do, ain't it?"

Charity pleaded with her eyes, but saw no response in the faces of the men. In panic, she rose and moved away from them, wading into shallower water and exposing more of herself. Undecided, she turned back to face them, crouching low in the water and trying to hide her nudity with her hands.

Reuben rode his gelding down into the creek and moved it over near Charity, grinning down at her. "Go ahead, get your clothes, we won't stop you."

"She's just a kid, Reuben," Sarge told him.

"If you don't want in on this, why don't you just go set under that tree for a bit?" Ayers said to Sarge, moving his pony down onto the other side of Charity. "But I ain't leaving till I seen this filly out of water."

Charity saw his lips make the words and got the sense of it. She did not know what to do. The men were all around her now. Then Ayers began moving his mount toward her, forcing her toward shallow water. She moved awkwardly away from him, and fell backwards into the shallow water. The water was very transparent now, and they got a good look at her. She stumbled to her feet, trying to cover herself, and then turned and splashed out of the stream toward her clothes. But Ayers got there first, and moved his horse between her and her clothing.

Charity was on dry land now and completely nude, and the two men were looking down on her nakedness from both sides.

"Not bad," Reuben said, watching her as she turned from one of them to the other.

"She'll do," Ayers said harshly.

Charity made a break for the trees and the camp beyond, but Ayers met her at the tree line, his pony almost knocking her down, his eyes devouring her every movement. Charity was in a wild panic now, and was making small grunting noises in her throat, the only sound of which she was capable. Her long dark hair flowed loosely over milky shoulders, and she looked good to the two men who were harassing her. Ayers dismounted and moved toward her.

"Where you think you're going, honey?"

Charity turned from him and almost stumbled into the thick-set Reuben, who had also dismounted. His evil grin made the panic rise even further in her chest. Turning again, she bolted headlong into the arms of Willis Ayers.

Charity was making the sounds again, and when Ayers grabbed her nudity and held it to him, she struggled fiercely and clawed at his face, her eyes like a cornered mustang's. Ayers just laughed aloud and held on and enjoyed it. Reuben moved up behind the girl then, and ran his hand over her flank as he would have if he were buying a horse. Finally Charity succumbed to weakness and shock, and slipped to the grassy bank exhausted. She lay on her back there then, staring up at them helplessly. Reuben nodded to Ayers, and they both began unbuckling their gunbelts. Sarge stood his mount in the stream, watching silently while his dun gelding drank. Now Reuben was kneeling over the girl, and Ayers was holding her arms. Sarge could hear the muffled, hoarse cries from the girl's throat as he walked his mount over to the trees. He dismounted there and walked through the trees until he could see the wagon clearly. While the girl thing was happening, he might at least take a look to see if the wagon seemed worth robbing.

Sarge stood behind a thick-trunked cottonwood and scanned the wagon camp. Even from here he could hear nothing of what was going on at the creek bank. As he watched, a middle-aged man with a paunch and a lined, sagging face came around the wagon and walked to the fire. He had pulled a pair of pants on, but the suspenders hung down at his sides and his belly and chest were covered only by a faded set of long red underwear. He moved to the fire and took the pot of coffee off.

"All right, Uriah!" he said loudly toward the wagon. "Move your freight, boy. We got to make it to Clancy this morning. And get that sister of yours up from the creek. I want something to eat."

Sarge squinted hard across the open space between them and saw a gold watch chain hanging from the professor's pants pocket. He glanced at the lettering on the wagon. Yes, this character just might have some money stashed away somewhere. Anyway, it would be worth finding out.

As he was making that decision, a young man climbed out of the wagon, a tall skinny lad, with sleep in his eyes and uncombed hair. He did not look much older than the girl at the creek. He went to a bucket of water to splash his face wet, and Sarge knew that very soon he would be coming down to the creek for the girl.

"What's it look like?"

Sarge turned at the sound of Reuben's voice. Reuben had walked his mount up behind Sarge, apparently through with the girl. The tails of the sweaty shirt were hanging out at his waist.

"We probably ought to see what they got," Sarge told him. "Where's Ayers?"

"He'll be along directly," Reuben grinned. "Say, you ought to try that, Sarge. You're missing something."

Sarge grunted. "While you two was playing, the men at the wagon was getting up. Now the young one is going to head down to the creek after the girl. We better move in now if we're going to."

They turned at Ayers' approach. He had placed a cavalry trooper's cap on his long head and had a glistening sparkle in his usually cold eyes. Sarge noticed that the knuckles of his right hand were bloody.

"You ready now for a little work?" Reuben said, laughing a dirty laugh in his throat.

"Yeah," Ayers said huskily. Sarge noticed the difference in his face and did not like what he saw there. "I'm ready."

"Okay. Let's see what the professor's got for sale," Reuben said to them.

The three mounted up and rode slowly to the camp. When they got halfway across the clearing, Uriah spotted them and stopped in the middle of toweling his face off. A moment later Ludwig jerked up quickly at the sound of the horses, surprise on his face.

Ludwig studied the three briefly, and then his eyes glanced past them to the trees and creek. "Well, good morning, strangers. Professor Ludwig at your service. Do you come for medical help or advice? You name a malady, and we cure it."

"We ain't got nothing wrong with us, old man," Reuben said, leaning forward onto his saddlehorn and making the leather under him squeak.

Ayers and Sarge had moved up to form a semicircle around the fire, where the professor stood uncertainly. Uriah stood at the wagon a few feet away, scared. He did not like the looks of these riders.

"Well, then, perhaps we can offer you a cup of coffee," the professor said genially, watching their faces closely. "Say, you didn't happen to see a girl down at the creek when you rode up?"

Ayers laughed in his throat.

"She's there, medicine man," Reuben said.

"And we're already acquainted," Ayers told him, grinning a hard grin at the professor.

"A pretty little thing," Reuben added.

The professor glanced past them again, his face now somber. "You better get down there and bring her back over here," he said slowly to Uriah.

"Yes, sir," Uriah said. He started around the riders.

"Hold it right there," Reuben said to him.

"Huh?" Uriah said.

"You heard me, boy," Reuben said harshly.

Ayers casually slid the Winchester rifle out of its scabbard and dismounted from his horse. Uriah stepped back a pace, eyeing him.

"Did you do anything to Charity?" Ludwig said loudly, his face turning suddenly red in anger.

Ayers turned and let the rifle point errantly at the professor, and the professor's eyes changed.

"The girl's all right," Sarge lied, his eyes hard under a dirty Stetson. "We're just poor discharged soldiers trying to make our way home, professor. And we thought you might want to contribute to the cause."

Professor Ludwig scanned the hard faces and wished he had the pistol in the wagon. "Contribute?" he said weakly. "Are you thieves?"

Reuben laughed again. His thick face, with its small eyes and stubble of beard, was as ugly as a steer's rump. "What you hiding in that wagon, professor? You got any money hid in with that worthless hog-wash?"

"You picked the wrong people, mister," Ludwig said. "We have nothing but our wares. We are dirt poor."

Reuben dismounted and walked over to Ludwig. When he got there, he raised his knee viciously and kicked Ludwig in the groin. The professor yelled in anguish and fell to his knees beside the fire, gritting his teeth in pain.

"We ain't got nothing!" Uriah yelled suddenly. "Just leave us alone!" He started toward Ludwig, but Ayers intercepted him and swung the stock of the rifle hard against Uriah's face. The impact cracked Uriah's cheekbone and slammed him to the ground, where he lay bleeding and moaning.

"Now you going to tell us where your money is hid?" Reuben said to Ludwig.

"Just a few dollars," the professor said, grunting it out. "That's all. It's here." He emptied a trousers pocket and a few coins spilled onto the ground.

Reuben looked hard at it. "You expect us to believe that?" he said. "You with a fancy wagon like this? Come on, professor, don't play with me."

Reuben kicked the professor's thigh, knocking the older man off balance and sending him onto his side in the dirt near the fire. Ludwig yelled again, but offered no more help to them.

Sarge now dismounted grumblingly and walked to the wagon. "If there's anything in here, I'll find it," he said. As he strode past Uriah, that young man was just struggling to his feet. Sarge hauled off and struck him across the face, knocking him onto his back again, then moved on to the wagon.

While Sarge ransacked the wagon, smashing bottles of medicine and tearing up the interior of the place, Ludwig listened and his heart sunk. Then he looked at the trees again. "Don't hurt Charity," he mumbled. "She doesn't deserve anything more bad. Please don't hurt Charity."

"We'll kill her, old man, if you don't level with us," Reuben told him harshly, in his pebbly voice. "And you can count that as a promise."

"Oh, God in heaven!" the professor said.

Sarge climbed down from the wagon with a disgruntled look on his square, mustached face. "If he's got money, he's got it well hid," he said to Reuben. "I say we move on. It ain't worth the effort."

Reuben looked over him. "We don't know that, do we?" he said.

Reuben turned back to Ludwig. "Now, you tell us the truth, old man, or Ayers there will kill the boy. Then we'll kill the girl."

"I told you," Ludwig pleaded with him. "We haven't made enough to buy food, since we left Dodge. We're down on our luck."

Reuben's little deep-set eyes squinted down even smaller. "I just don't believe that, medicine man," he said. He nodded to Ayers.

Ayers turned back to Uriah Jenkins just as the young man was awkwardly attempting to stand for the second time. He was dazed, and his face was bloody, with his cheek crushed in. He had just stood up, when Ayers aimed the rifle at his chest and pulled the trigger at close range.

The rifle roared in Uriah's ears and exploded in his chest. The slug hit him just above the heart and tore a chunk out of his back as it passed through. The force of it picked him off his feet and hurled him backwards against the bright-colored wagon, where he made a crimson mark on its side before he slipped to the ground. He had been dead before he hit the wagon.

"What kind of men are you?" professor Ludwig said in a half whisper as he stared at the body of Uriah.

"Pick him up," Reuben said to Sarge.

Sarge roughly pulled Ludwig to his feet and held him. Reuben walked over close to him. "We're this kind of men," he said. He threw a big fist into Ludwig's side, breaking a rib. Then he threw several more punches into the body and face of the older man, while Sarge held him. In a moment, the professor was a limp, bloody mass. Sarge dropped him and he slumped to his knees.

"Well?" Reuben said loudly, his face dark with a rage that was getting out of hand. He did not really believe, now, that there was money in the wagon, but he had to punish this man for wasting his time. That was what it was all about, but he did not know it himself. Reuben did not have the capacity to think, just feel.

"Why don't you let it go?" Sarge said, seeing the rage build in Reuben's broad face.

"Like hell," Reuben said hotly. He bent over the professor now. "Let's see whether this makes you talk." He pushed Ludwig over toward the fire, face down.

"No!" Ludwig yelled.

"You like heat?" Reuben said in a taut voice, strained and hoarse, the veins standing out blue in his thick neck.

"I'm telling you—the truth," the professor gasped.

Ayers stood nearby with the rifle under his arm, grinning tightly. Sarge, his hard face watching straight-lined, knew it was no use talking to Reuben now. He was past that.

"We'll see," Reuben said to Ludwig. His big hand pushed the professor's face down right into the fire and held it there.

The professor began screaming almost immediately, and struggling violently under Reuben's grasp. But Reuben's iron grip was too much for him, and he could not extricate his face from the flames. The screaming continued, and then there was a coughing and gasping, and when the professor's face began turning black from the fire, Sarge turned and walked away. Ayers stared fascinated at it.

In just a few minutes it was all over. Reuben's arm had the hair singed, and there were minor burns on the hand that held the professor's head, but Reuben did not notice. When he finally released the professor, the man collapsed face down into the fire. Reuben stood up then, still staring hard and unseeing at the lifeless form of the professor. He blinked a couple of times, and seemed to regain his sanity.

Ayers had picked up a big bottle of cure-all from

the back of the wagon. He now walked over to the professor with it and uncorked the bottle. He poured the contents onto the professor's head, killing the fire and the stench from the professor.

"See if that helps, professor," he said.

The broad man called Sarge moved over to the fire now and pulled the professor clear of it. He turned the man over and grimaced when he saw the face. "Well, you killed him," he said to Reuben. "Now can we get out of here?"

"The ornery old bastard," Reuben said, seemingly himself again. "He shouldn't have—"

Reuben looked up in mid-sentence, his eyes focusing out over the tall grass. Ayers and Sarge followed his gaze, and they saw what he had heard. A rider coming toward them from over a small hill. It looked like a cowboy, probably from a ranch nearby.

Ayers raised the rifle and trained it on the rider.

"Put that thing down!" Sarge said. "Throw the boy into the wagon while I put a tarpaulin over this corpse."

Reuben looked from the rider to Sarge. "Yeah. That's right, Ayers. Ain't you got no brains at all? He'll have friends nearby somewhere. You want to bring them all down on us?"

By the time the cowpoke rode up to the wagon, they had hidden the two bodies. The cowpoke rode up warily, his right hand near a gun on his hip.

"A couple of us heard a shot over this way," he said as he edged closer to them. "Everything all right here?"

"Everything's just fine," Reuben said in his hard voice.

"We just rode up overselves," Sarge added quickly. "The owner of the wagon ain't around. We fired off a round to see if we could raise him from over the hill. We wanted a cup of his coffee."

The cowpoke saw the broken bottles at the rear of the wagon, on the ground there, and the suspicious-looking tarpaulin at the side of the vehicle. He shifted his gaze to the rifle under Ayers' arm. "Well, I reckon the good professor is nearby somewhere. If you didn't get the coffee, we got a camp about a mile over that hill back there."

"Much obliged, cowboy," Sarge said. "But we're just about to hit the trail."

"Suit yourself," the cowboy said. "I'll just be heading back then."

He started to turn his mount. He was suspicious, but he wanted to get out from under their guns. But before he could turn, he saw the figure moving out of the trees and toward them. His jaw dropped open and he stared hard. The others turned and looked too.

It was Charity Jenkins. She had just emerged from the trees, still naked. She staggered toward them numbly, her body beaten and bruised. Her throat had been cut by Ayers, but the wound had not yet been fatal. Blood ran from the cut across her throat, down onto her bruised and scratched body. Her mouth was working, and the sounds were coming from her throat.

"By Jesus!" the cowboy said, his mouth suddenly dry.

Sarge pulled his Colt and the cowboy heard it, but too late. Sarge's revolver banged in the morning air, and the cowboy was hit in the side just as his hand was going for his own gun. Then Ayers' rifle roared, and the cowpoke was torn from his mount. The frightened animal reared and bolted, raising a gallop toward the hill it had just come over. Ayers took careful aim on the horse as it ran, though, and the rifle crashed again and he broke the animal's back in the middle of a stride. It plunged heavily onto its nose and did a flip on the grassy hill, landing on its side.

Reuben walked over to the cowboy, who was lying on the ground moaning. Reuben drew his revolver, pointed it at the cowpoke's head, and fired, tearing a hole in the cowpoke's skull. The figure jumped and was still.

"Let's get out of here," Sarge said. He went to his horse and mounted it.

"Not just yet," Reuben said. He turned to the steadily advancing Charity "You got to learn to finish a job when you start on it," he said to Ayers. He aimed his Colt at the girl as she neared them, and fired again, at the head. Charity hit the ground just short of camp.

"Come on now, Reuben," Sarge said from his mount. "There will be people here."

Reuben walked over to the wagon and stood looking at it with his hands on his hips. Then he moved up against it, his big hands pushing against its side. The wagon moved, tipped slowly away from Reuben under his brute strength, and then suddenly fell over heavily onto its side with a loud crash and a raising of dust. Reuben turned from it then, walked over to the body of the professor, and ripped the tarpaulin off it. He kicked the body savagely, twice. Then he went to his gelding and mounted it. Ayers followed suit.

"Let's ride," Reuben Latimer told his comrades, and he dug his spurs savagely into the gelding's sides.

★2★

O'Brien's luck had not been good on this hunting trip. He had been trailing buffalo for years, but this year was the worst by far. There were only two big herds left in all of Texas, and a few up north scattered over a couple thousand miles, and the shaggies were getting as hard to locate as bankers in heaven.

O'Brien thought on that as his big rawboned frame jerked along now on the seat of the gut-wagon, behind the bony flanks of a long-eared mule. The hunter wore a handlebar mustache and long hair under a trail-colored Stetson, and he was dressed in rawhides and stovepipe boots. The rawhides had taken on the odor of the buffalo he hunted.

Behind the wagon O'Brien's appaloosa stallion moved gracefully, keeping pace with the mule. O'Brien's hunting rifles were on its irons.

Up ahead on the trail a few miles, O'Brien would, he knew, have to make a decision. A fork in the road offered the choice of riding to Fort Griffin with its big market for hides, but also with its stiff competition from other hunters, or heading toward the small town of Clancy with a small hide market, but possibly no other hunters there to drive the price down. He was considering this matter when he looked up and saw the two wagons break over the crest of a hill about a half mile away.

O'Brien reined up and focused on the wagons, which were moving toward him on the trail. They were freight wagons and were probably carrying hides from Clancy or Fort Griffin. There was one man on each wagon.

O'Brien watched the wagons for a moment, then climbed off his wagon and walked to the appaloosa. He slid his Winchester rifle from its saddle scabbard. Then he checked it for ammunition, and climbed back aboard the wagon and laid the rifle on the seat beside him. Mule skinners were a rough lot, drifters at heart usually, and O'Brien had found that a man kept his distance from them. The wagons were very near now, so O'Brien just sat and waited for them to reach him, knowing there would be an exchange of communication. When they rolled to a stop alongside, the mule skinner on the front wagon spoke to him.

"I see you're a hunter," the man said. He was a barrel-chested, dirty man with a beard and he was looking past O'Brien to the hides in O'Brien's wagon.

"That's right," O'Brien said. "You heading north with hides?"

"Going to Dodge with them," the man said, spitting into the dust beneath him.

The second mule skinner, a short ugly man, hopped off his wagon and came up to join the exchange. He did not smile when he spoke. "How's the shaggies running, hunter?" he said. He wore a gun on his hip, as did his comrade, and O'Brien did not like the tone of his voice.

"Scarce," O'Brien answered.

The big man disembarked too, moving over to O'Brien's wagon to take a look at the hides. He grunted. "You ain't got much here. You want to sell them?"

"That depends on the price," O'Brien said.

"Well, they sure ain't much," the big man said.

O'Brien knew trade talk when he heard it. "Well, maybe I better just take them on to Fort Griffin," he said.

"You don't have to get stiff-backed about it," the ugly man said. "You ain't heard our price yet."

"If you're making an offer, do it," O'Brien said acidly.

The big man looked at the hides again, and then walked up to the front of O'Brien's wagon and leaned on his mule. "It's too much, but I'll give you twenty dollars for the whole bunch."

"You better take it and run, buffalo man," the short ugly man said, grinning. "You won't get no better one."

O'Brien looked from the big man to the ugly one. He did not like them or their offer. "I think I'll see if I can better that in town," he said firmly.

The short ugly man sighed heavily and gave his partner a look. Then he turned back to O'Brien.

"Buffalo man, you don't seem to get the idea. We want them hides of yours, you see, and you can figure that we mean to have them."

O'Brien grunted, unimpressed. "For a fair price, you can have the batch of them. But not otherwise." He hefted the reins to leave.

Suddenly, and without warning, the ugly man beside O'Brien's seat pulled his gun. He raised it deliberately and aimed it at O'Brien. "You just lost your chance to sell them hides, mister," he said to O'Brien.

O'Brien narrowed his cold blue eyes on the ugly man. His hand had dropped down near his rifle, with the reins in it. "How are you going to tell this back in Clancy?" he said.

The husky man now pulled his gun, too. "We'll think of something," he said, grinning. He turned and aimed his gun at the mule's head, and shot it.

The mule jerked violently and fell onto its side, kicked for a moment, and was still. It had dragged the wagon sidewise with it, and busted the left front wheel off the axle, almost throwing O'Brien off the seat. As he grabbed the seat to keep his balance, he also moved his other hand onto the Winchester. When it was quiet again, O'Brien looked hard at the dead mule. It had cost him a good price recently and was a good mule. He looked from the mule to his busted gut-wagon, and then back to the man who had done the shooting.

"Mule skinner, that was a mistake," he said, his voice a low growl now.

"I don't think so," the husky man named Harley told him. "Now you *can't* move them hides to market. Get off the wagon."

"Yeah," the ugly man near O'Brien said. "And throw that rifle down first. Easy like."

"Sure," O'Brien said. He turned and swung his legs off the seat, in preparation to jumping down.

The ugly man was very close. "I said, the rifle first," he said to O'Brien.

"Oh. Anything you say." O'Brien grabbed the rifle with his right hand and, before the mule skinner knew what he was doing, started it in a big arc toward the man's head, grabbing it with the other hand as it came around.

The ugly man's only reaction was to try to duck away from what was happening, but he was not fast enough. The rifle swung hard into his face, O'Brien coming off the seat simultaneously with the swinging rifle, and there was a dull crunching as the ugly man felt the barrel jam against him, smashing teeth and bone.

O'Brien's feet hit the ground just as a muffled yell came from the mule skinner's mangled mouth. The gun he held exploded, the slug missing O'Brien and burying itself in the wood of the wagon.

The other man fired awkwardly past his companion just as the ugly man was crashing heavily to the ground, and while O'Brien was adjusting his grip on the Winchester, slipping into a crouch, and bringing the rifle to bear on the husky man. The shot tore O'Brien's Stetson off his head but missed him. O'Brien fired just a half-second later, the rifle roaring loudly in their ears, and the slug hit the husky man in the shoulder, spinning him in a tight circle and throwing him down against O'Brien's dead mule. From that position, he turned to face the big man again, still holding the revolver. He aimed it again at O'Brien, more carefully this time. But O'Brien fired the Winchester again, hitting the man's gun arm and flinging the revolver out of his grasp. He yelled loudly and grabbed the arm.

"You got us!" he said then to O'Brien, breathing hard and grunting with pain. "You got us, don't kill us!"

"Why not?" he said in that deep growl. He shucked a shell from the chamber of the rifle and re-cocked.

O'Brien saw a movement out of the corner of his eye. The ugly man, a bloody mess, had spotted his gun near him on the ground, and was reaching for it now. Crimson covered his lower face, and his front teeth had been spit onto the ground around him.

Just as he found the gun with his hand, O'Brien moved over to him and kicked him hard in the side, breaking two ribs. The man groaned loudly and collapsed onto his back in severe pain.

O'Brien stood over him grimly, the Winchester held loosely under his arm. "I ought to kill both of you," he said in the low, hard voice. "But the plain truth of it is, you ain't worth killing."

"My arm is broke," the husky man muttered through clenched teeth.

The ugly man, who was at the moment a whole lot uglier than he had been before, tried to say something to O'Brien in defense of their lives, but could not work his jaw. His eyes had a different look now and he was in fact a changed man. He had found humility in a hurry.

O'Brien picked up his Stetson and settled it onto his shaggy head, then walked to the gunshot mule skinner and ripped a money pouch off the man's belt. O'Brien took out some gold coins in payment for the hides, wagon and mule. "You made your sale after all," he said. "The mule and wagon is yours, too. I only took a fair sale price. Any questions?"

The husky man shook his head desperately.

"That's good," O'Brien said, throwing the pouch into the dirt near the man. "Now I'm going to tell you something. If I ever see either one of you two hauling hides again, anywhere, you won't get off so easy. I'll make you think this was a Sunday prayer meeting."

Neither man was in any shape to answer him. He went then to the appaloosa which was still picketed to the back of his gut-wagon, and untied it and mounted up. He steered the horse between the men as he left, without giving them another glance. They, however, sitting in the dirt bleeding, mashed and white-faced, ruefully watched his receding back move away from them until he was out of sight.

When O'Brien reached the fork in the trail later, he had already made the decision to take the trail in to Clancy. He needed to buy a mule and wagon now, and he intended to report to the freight company on the kind of men they had hired and to set them straight on the sale, in case their money was involved. As it was to turn out, his decision to take the left side of that fork was to cause him considerably more trouble this bright morning than he had already had, and was to be one of the gravest mistakes he had ever made.

It was more than an hour later when O'Brien

crested a ridge and saw the overturned medicine drummer's wagon down near the creek, just off the trail. He reined up slowly, and took the scene in at a distance of several hundred yards. All he could see from there was the wagon, lying on its side, and the team of horses still picketed at the trees beyond, and the strange dead look of the encampment. It looked very much like the owner of that wagon had seen serious trouble. And if there was something O'Brien did not need, it was more trouble right now. But he could not just ride by.

O'Brien slipped the Winchester out of its saddle scabbard and checked the ammunition in it, then spurred the appaloosa into a walk down the slope toward the wagon.

He did not see the body of the girl Charity until he was within a hundred yards. He moved up to fifty, slowly, watching around him now, not liking the quiet of the place. The girl lay sprawled awkwardly at the edge of the encampment, starkly nude, blood-spattered, with the back of her head blown off. O'Brien walked the mount on into the camp then, and when he rounded the end of the fallen wagon, he saw the arm of Uriah Jenkins sticking out of the back curtains, and the professor's body near the front wheels.

O'Brien narrowed his eyes on the results of the massacre. He had not seen anything like this since a man named Duke Pritchard had killed Ethan Tobias and his whole family in a cold-blooded slaughter and O'Brien had had to go after Pritchard.

O'Brien dismounted and picketed the stallion to a rear wheel of the overturned wagon, then walked over to the corpse of the professor. He looked at the battered body and the charred head, and his lips drew into straight lines.

"Damn," he said softly.

He turned then and went to the boy at the back of the wagon, pulling the curtain back. He felt of the boy's pulse, then turned the body over and saw the hole in its back. The appaloosa whinnied nervously, scenting the blood.

Last of all, O'Brien went and looked at the corpse of the girl. He bent over it and studied it for a long moment, and an anger built in his chest against the men who could have done to her what he saw.

Heavily, O'Brien returned to the wagon. Maybe there would be a shovel there somewhere and he could bury the bodies before they began to stink. There were already green blowflies laying eggs inside the girl's skull.

O'Brien laid his rifle up against the wagon, and pulled the curtain back again and dragged the body of the boy Uriah out onto the ground. Then he stepped into the overturned vehicle, crouching low, and began looking around inside. He had been in there only a moment when he heard the sound outside. It was riders.

By the time O'Brien got back outside, the five men had reined up around the wagon. He would not have been caught by surprise, except that his movement in the wagon covered their approach. He looked around at the five faces, and saw the shock in them at what they had just seen when they rode up. The man closest to O'Brien wore a badge on his shirt and it glinted brightly in the morning sun. He looked from the bodies to O'Brien with a deep scowl on his swarthy face. O'Brien moved to reclaim his rifle, but a man beside the lawman pulled a gun.

"Hold it right there, mister," he said.

O'Brien stopped and turned to face them again, only a pace away from the rifle. Well, he thought, if they were a posse, he would not need the rifle. He would explain that he had just arrived on the scene himself, and they would understand

"What did you find in there?" the lawman asked O'Brien.

O'Brien did not like the sound of his voice. It was loaded with sarcasm and prejudice, and it sounded like an accusation. O'Brien looked at the other men again, and their faces were still grim from viewing the bodies.

"I was looking for a shovel to bury the bodies," O'Brien said. "I arrived just before you."

The sheriff, a Mexican-American named Castillo, glared at O'Brien with open hatred and contempt. "I'll just bet you did," he said acidly. He turned to the man who had drawn the gun. "Hold that gun on him."

The sheriff dismounted then, and went from one corpse to the other, shaking his head. The other men followed him with their grim eyes, silent and brooding. When the sheriff walked back over to O'Brien, O'Brien did not like the look in his dark face.

"This here is about the bloodiest thing I've seen in a lot of years lawing," the sheriff said to O'Brien. "That girl over there—"

"I know what you mean, sheriff," O'Brien said.

"Don't hand me that, you scum!" the sheriff said

harshly to O'Brien. "You was part of this, and you know it."

O'Brien's eyes narrowed down on Castillo. He looked into his hard eyes, and he knew that the sheriff really thought he was somehow involved. "Now just a minute—" O'Brien said.

The men were dismounting one at a time, slowly, and moving toward O'Brien and the wagon. They were in a mean mood.

"Why don't we just hang him right here, sheriff?" one of them said softly.

"Hang him, hell!" another said in a loud, hoarse voice. "That's too damn good for the likes of him. He deserves to die slow, like she did." He waved an arm at the dead girl.

The man with the gun on O'Brien looked as if he might pull the trigger any minute.

"Maybe before you go off half-cocked," O'Brien said, keeping his voice calm, "you ought to hear my side of it."

"Don't let him talk his way out of this," a third man said.

The sheriff had calmed down some. "Don't appear you could have much to say, in the face of the evidence," he said.

"Evidence?" O'Brien said.

"That's right. We caught you red-handed going through the wagon, didn't we? I figure you stayed behind the others to make one last search for the professor's cash. Am I right?"

"Behind what others?" O'Brien said to him. "Whoever done this was gone when I got here. I just told you that."

"You're part of the Reuben Latimer gang,"

sheriff Castillo persisted in his hard monotone, with the slight accent. "That's plain as the nose on your face. We expected him to recruit a gunman or two before he left this area, and you're a gun he hired, ain't you?"

O'Brien sighed heavily. He had had a notion he should have ridden on past this wagon, when he saw it from the hill. But he had thought somebody might need help. Now, he did. He thought back to the incident with the mule skinners, and wondered how much could happen to a man in one morning.

"I'm a buffalo hunter," O'Brien said to Castillo. "My name is O'Brien. You can check it out in Dodge. I never heard of this Reuben Latimer."

"Hang the bastard now, Castillo," somebody said.

Castillo grimaced. "As you can see, you got to do better than that, mister. Your set of tracks come from the trail right alongside the tracks of three other mounts. I can identify one of the other three definitely as belonging to Latimer's horse, since I been tracking him for two days through this county. And then there's the matter of that Winchester standing there."

"What about it?" O'Brien said.

"The hole in the boy's chest there was made with a rifle, and my guess is it was a Winchester." Castillo moved to O'Brien's rifle, and picked it up. O'Brien was held in place by the posse deputy's gun.

"Now, you want to tell me that the gun ain't been fired?" Castillo said. Without waiting for an answer, he smelled the barrel of the rifle, and a tight grin came onto his face.

"Sure it's been fired," O'Brien said slowly, knowing suddenly how bad it all looked. "I had a fracas earlier, on the trail, with some mule skinners that tried to rob me. I fired the rifle then, and wounded one of them. It's less than two hours from here. Go check it out and you'll probably find them."

The sheriff grinned wider. "And I suppose you, a hunter, just happen to be out here without no equipment or hides, and no partner, because of some equally good reason?"

O'Brien hesitated a moment, knowing now that nothing he said would be believed. "That's right," he finally said. "The hide men killed my mule and I left the whole rig back there. As for a partner, I hunt alone."

"He's a lying murderer, sheriff!" a deputy said.

"Lynch him right here!"

O'Brien looked around at them and knew his chances were slim if he started something. There were too many. But maybe it was better than letting this go the way it was.

The man with the drawn gun now pointed it squarely at O'Brien's chest. "Why take the time to hang him?" he said. "This is easier."

There was little doubt in O'Brien's mind that he intended to pull the trigger. And the sheriff would react too slowly to stop him, even if he wanted to. So O'Brien took the only course of action available to him.

O'Brien dived sidewise toward the ground, between the sheriff and the man with the gun. The deputy fired, as O'Brien expected, and hit O'Brien in the left arm. As O'Brien hit the ground, he drew the hunting knife which he always carried in his stove-pipe boot, and, as he rolled to his knee, threw it at the deputy. It thudded hard into the man's low side, making his eyes go round before he dropped. In the meantime, two other deputies had drawn their guns and were trying to make O'Brien their target. However, O'Brien now dived at the sheriff, as the sheriff raised O'Brien's own rifle toward him. O'Brien knocked the gun away with a big hand and went crashing against the sheriff, driving him into the overturned wagon. O'Brien twisted as he fell against the rear wheel, putting the sheriff briefly between himself and the other men, causing them to hold their fire. O'Brien now pulled the rifle hard up against the sheriff's throat, and held it there.

"I'll kill him with this," he said to them, "if you don't drop the guns."

Two of the three, looking down at the dead deputy on the ground with the knife sticking out of him dropped their guns. The third one fired wildly at O'Brien's head, missing both O'Brien and Castillo by inches, and then dived at them like an insane man.

Unwittingly, the man had taken the most effective action possible. He was on the other men in a fury, tearing and hitting at O'Brien with the gun, and causing O'Brien to divert his attention from the sheriff. O'Brien managed to knock the gun from the man's grasp, but then the sheriff had squirmed free from the pull of the rifle, and dropped out of O'Brien's grasp. He scrambled a short distance away while O'Brien hauled off and threw a fist into the deputy's ribs, cracking them like kindling wood and hurling the man to the ground on his back.

O'Brien then kicked out toward the sheriff as another man jumped on him, and O'Brien's boot caught the sheriff in the side and threw him back to the ground.

The new man on O'Brien was bigger, and had caught O'Brien by surprise. He hit O'Brien hard twice, staggering the big man back against the wheel again, and then they were locked in brutal combat. The last man, however, had regained his gun in the confusion, and moved around behind O'Brien, and just as O'Brien was about to unleash another big fist into the face of the deputy who was slugging it out with him, the man with the gun brought the barrel of it down hard on the back of O'Brien's head.

O'Brien's vision went black for a moment and he hit the ground. When he hit, he could see again, and struggled to his knees. The pistol came down again, though, and he went down a second time. The big deputy who had been slugging with O'Brien then grabbed the gun from the man with the busted ribs, and aimed it at O'Brien's head.

"If you won't kill him, I will!" he said, breathlessly.

The sheriff, regaining his feet unsteadily, yelled at the fourth deputy, who had just stood wide-eyed staring at the fight, watching O'Brien as if the man were a wild animal. "Get that rifle he dropped!" he said.

The man looked at the sheriff, and then moved in toward O'Brien and the rifle.

O'Brien was trying to focus again when the big deputy aimed the revolver at his head. O'Brien did not even see the gun, but he saw the boots of the man standing near him, so he threw himself at them.

O'Brien came at the big man so fast that he missed O'Brien when he fired and hit the deputy with the busted ribs in the leg. The man yelled loudly as O'Brien hit the big deputy and threw him to the ground. The big deputy was amazed that the man he had thought half dead a moment before was now on him again, like a cougar.

As O'Brien smashed his big fists into the deputy, breaking the man's nose and tearing his mouth, the fourth deputy moved in timidly and grabbed the Winchester, jumping back quickly with it. Once he had the long gun in hand, he was much bolder. He raised it quickly and aimed it at O'Brien's head.

O'Brien had knocked the big deputy senseless, and now turned like an enraged animal toward the man with the rifle. Seeing that face turn toward him, the man almost lost his courage. But he stood his ground long enough to find the trigger assembly on the rifle. He breathlessly squeezed on the trigger.

"Wait," the sheriff said.

"Huh?" the deputy said, glancing with fear-filled eyes briefly at Castillo.

"I said, hold it. I want this man alive."

"You better kill him, sheriff," the deputy said, licking dry lips, and seeing O'Brien's cold, savage eyes.

O'Brien knelt there, watching the barrel of the rifle. The man could not miss at this distance.

The sheriff, recovering now from O'Brien's assault on him earlier, drew his own gun and trained it on O'Brien's chest. "No, we got him now," Castillo said, not sounding so sure himself. "Now you just squat right there, mister, or I'll blow your heart right out of your back."

With the two guns zeroed in on him, O'Brien decided finally that they had him. But he never quit watching for some opportunity to renew his assault. Around them on the ground lay the dead man with the knife in him, the man with the busted ribs and gunshot leg, and the big deputy whose face was busted up and bloody from O'Brien's fists. He was just coming to, mumbling something between thick lips. The man who had been shot by mistake was gritting his teeth in pain.

At a motion from the sheriff, the man with the rifle moved cautiously around in back of O'Brien, while the sheriff stepped forward.

"You ain't no man, you're an animal," Castillo was saying to O'Brien as he moved forward and pointed the gun at O'Brien's heart. "And you're going to learn how animals is treated, before I'm through with you."

The sheriff looked past O'Brien, who was seeing double now, and made another head motion to the deputy with the rifle. O'Brien turned slightly just in time to see the barrel of the long gun swing down onto the side of his head. He could not react in time. The length of metal crunched against his skull hard, making bright lights explode in his head, and knocking him onto his side in the dirt. He lay there then unmoving, in a cold blackness shot through with bright splotches of pain, and twice he felt a boot crash into his side as he lay there helpless, then he felt nothing.

When he came to a short time later, he was bound hand and foot, and the sheriff and his unhurt deputy, with the help of the big one with the battered face, had righted the medicine drummer's wagon, thrown all the bodies in it, including that of the deputy O'Brien had killed in self defense, and had hitched the team to the wagon. O'Brien struggled onto his elbow and looked around grunting with the effort. He felt as if a wagon had rolled over his head. His body hurt whenever he moved. He was still seeing double. As he tried to focus, Castillo walked over to him.

"Well, he ain't dead after all." He came and bent over O'Brien, confident now that O'Brien was tied up.

O'Brien grunted and looked at the two sheriffs leaning over him and hated both of them. He tried hard to focus them down to one, but could not.

"What's that you said?" Castillo said.

O'Brien stared at him.

"You ain't quite so juicy now, are you?" the sheriff said. "Oh, you caused me some trouble, all right. But now we got you, ain't we, O'Brien, or whoever you are?"

"Go to hell," O'Brien managed.

The sheriff laughed a soft laugh, then kicked O'Brien hard in the thigh. O'Brien grunted but made no other sound.

"I see all the juice ain't gone. Well, it will be, before it's all over for you, O'Brien. It's going to be rough. I can promise you that."

The healthy deputy walked up, the one who had hit O'Brien with the Winchester. "A man like that ought to get it slow," he said to Castillo.

"You hear him, O'Brien?" Castillo said. "The boys don't seem to like you very much. The ones that's left, that is. And you can figure that that's the way the people in Last Hope will feel when I bring you in today. So why don't you make it easy on yourself, and tell me where Reuben Latimer's headed?"

"I told you. I ain't one of them," O'Brien said.

Castillo grabbed O'Brien's long hair and held his face up. "When I get you behind bars, that stubborn streak won't last long," he said. "I got some plans for you."

The deputy spoke up then. "What you mean, sheriff?" he said. "He'll hang, won't he?"

Castillo looked over at him. "Eventually, yes. But I want Reuben Latimer and the rest of them deserters and murderers, too. And this one's going to tell me where they went. If I have to put him through hell to wring it out of him."

★3★

When the bizarre party arrived in Last Hope, where Castillo was the duly elected sheriff and the only law, the townsfolk gathered in the street to watch the procession pass by, and Castillo did not miss that opportunity to rile them against O'Brien. He had gotten hold of an old bear muzzle and strapped it to O'Brien's face, and wound a dozen lengths of rope around his chest and arms, and untied his feet and hobbled them, so he could make O'Brien walk behind the medicine wagon on a tether as they passed through the heart of the small village.

The bodies of the professor and the Jenkinses were displayed on the seat of the wagon, with a cloth thrown across the girl, and the dead deputy was thrown over a horse and became part of the parade also. The wounded and battered deputies rode grimly ahead of the wagon, with the dead deputy, while Castillo brought up the rear, prodding O'Brien with a stick, as if O'Brien were a mad dog.

When the onlookers found out that the man wearing the muzzle was charged with the gruesome murders, a few of them went wild and wanted to lynch O'Brien then and there, before the sheriff got him to the jail.

"Don't you worry none about it," Castillo told them solemnly. "This man will get what he deserves. And so will the others that was with him when this massacre took place."

Most of them were appeased, and relented. The father of the dead deputy, though, when he saw O'Brien, ran over to him with a singletree and brought it down across O'Brien's neck and back before anybody could stop him. O'Brien fell to the ground on his knees, stunned, and then was dragged for a short distance before the wagon team was stopped.

A couple of men came and took the singletree away from the man, as he stood there breathing hard and staring wildly at the fallen O'Brien.

"Murderer!" he yelled. "Cold-blooded fiend!"

O'Brien tried to regain his feet, and fell back to the ground. He had been lucky the man had not broken his neck with the weapon. He stared into the man's angry face, and then at the other faces around him. They came to towns and bound together for their common welfare and made laws and lawmen, and through all of it became something less than they had been before. O'Brien thought back to his decision to take the trail toward Clancy, and knew with a certainty that it was the single worst choice he had ever made.

O'Brien finally managed to stand, although he was very dizzy and weak, and the procession continued to the small jail. On the way, men and women alike threw insults at the man wearing the bear muzzle and who looked like a wild man, and children threw stones at him, but O'Brien was in no condition to care.

When they reached the adobe structure that passed for a jail, O'Brien was taken inside, thrown into the one cell like an animal, and locked up. No move was made to remove the muzzle or his bonds, which encircled him like a net.

O'Brien lay on his side looking through the bars groggily while the sheriff asked the people outside to leave. Finally, Castillo and the unharmed deputy returned inside the small place, which was divided into a cell and a kind of ante-room, and sat on a couple of hard chairs and discussed O'Brien.

"You can't just deputize a bunch of men for a posse, and take them out to something like we just saw, and then expect them to go back home and forget it," the man was saying to Castillo. "We maybe don't have no badges, but we got a stake in what happens to that—thing in the cage there. So does the rest of the town."

"I appreciate that," Castillo told him. "But taking this man out and hanging him this afternoon ain't in the best interests of this town. Reuben Latimer's the head of the octopus, and it's him we got to think about."

"He might not know where Latimer's headed," the deputy said.

"I'm betting that he does," the sheriff said grimly.

Castillo went over and unlocked the door to the cell. He went in, accompanied by the deputy. Castillo untied the ropes around O'Brien's chest, but left his wrists bound. He removed the hobbles from his ankles and, lastly, unstrapped the muzzle.

O'Brien watched them, saying nothing.

"You know, I think by now this hunter-turned-killer is beginning to see the kind of trouble he's in," Castillo said, as if speaking to his deputy. "Ain't that right, buffalo man?"

O'Brien grimaced. "You got to be hard of hearing, sheriff. You brought in the wrong man."

Castillo's face grew dark. "Latimer shot a man dead in these streets a little while ago. I don't know whether you was with him then or not, but it don't matter. You're going to tell me where he's gone."

"I told you I don't know Latimer," O'Brien said heavily.

Castillo became suddenly very angry. He nodded to the deputy, and that man came and drew his pistol and stood over O'Brien with it. He grinned for a moment, then brought the muzzle of the gun down onto O'Brien's head. O'Brien groaned and slumped onto his side.

"Now you want to talk?" Castillo said.

O'Brien pushed himself back up, an anger rising inside him again, one that he had little control over. "Damn you—!" he breathed.

"This is going to keep on until you start talking," Castillo told him. "So you might as well level with us now."

O'Brien was in a crouching position, on one knee. He watched the deputy hover over him with the gun. "Don't hit me again with that thing," he said in a low voice.

The deputy grinned nervously and flicked his gaze momentarily to Castillo. Castillo gave him the signal again. The deputy brought the pistol down again toward O'Brien's head. O'Brien ducked and the gun grazed the side of his head and struck his neck and shoulder. In the same instant, O'Brien got his feet under him and lunged at the deputy.

O'Brien's big frame hit the other man hard and they went sprawling through the open cell door and hit the floor beyond together. The deputy lost his gun and it skittered across the floor out of sight.

Castillo had moved away from the action and now grabbed for his own gun, watching O'Brien on his deputy, his hands still bound, swinging them together at the deputy's head. He connected and bone snapped in the deputy's nose and he yelled aloud in pain.

O'Brien lost his balance with the blow, and the deputy got away from him momentarily, trying to see his fallen pistol.

"Hold it, hunter!" Castillo yelled.

But O'Brien, on his feet finally, ignored the sheriff's voice and kicked the deputy in the side as he tried to get up off the floor, blood on the lower part of his face. Ribs cracked and the deputy yelled out again and hit the floor on his side. O'Brien was about to give him another one, when he felt the muzzle of Castillo's gun at the back of his head.

"Hold it right there, or you're a dead man."

O'Brien turned slowly to Castillo. "You keep your people off me," he said, still breathing hard.

"He— busted me up," the deputy was moaning, trying to get off the floor. He fell back onto his side and lay there, making sounds in his throat.

"You're a crazy man, hunter," Castillo said.

"Oh— God," the deputy gasped.

"You're a menace to civilized folks, there's no doubt about it," Castillo added. He waved his gun at him. "But we'll take care of that. Back inside, hunter."

Castillo rounded up three volunteers to guard the jail that night, after re-binding O'Brien's feet. The next morning early Castillo met with Mayor Hollis and a local justice of the peace called Old Necessity, in the back room of the feed store, and they discussed what to do with O'Brien.

"The man ought to be drawn and quartered," Old Necessity offered. He was a hard-looking old fellow in his sixties with white hair and beard and a rusty six-shooter hanging on his hip. He was well renowned in the area for his unusual methods of administering justice. He was no lawyer, in fact, had gone only to the third grade in a frontier school. So he decided the civil cases that came before him by the prudent application of "horse sense." When he held court, he always kept a mail-order catalogue on his desk, with a leather cover over it, to make it look like a law book.

"You should have let the mob have him," Hollis offered.

"If I did that, I'd never know where to find Reuben Latimer," Castillo said balefully.

"Are you still bucking for that marshal's badge in Clancy?" Hollis said, with a wry grin.

Castillo gave him a look. "That ain't the point. Latimer has made me and this whole county look bad. That don't set right with me."

"Well, it doesn't look like that buffalo man will tell you anything," Hollis said.

"And you'll have to feed him till the circuit judge comes," Old Necessity added. "Which could be a blue moon."

Castillo looked up at them. "That ain't what I got in mind. I got it in my head to go ahead and try him, right now."

"How?" Hollis asked.

Castillo jerked his thumb at Old Necessity. "With the judge here," he said caustically.

"Me? A criminal case?" the old fellow said. "The law says—"

"You don't know what the law says," Castillo said harshly. "Anyway, we can make our own law this time. We run this town."

"What's the point?" Hollis said. "Let the mob lynch him, if you want to hang him. But that won't find Latimer for you."

"I ain't going to hang him," Castillo said. "I got in mind sending him down to my old friend at Bradenville."

"The warden at the state prison?" Hollis asked.

Castillo nodded. Old Necessity grunted. "The Black Hole of Texas. A little bit of hell right here on earth."

"That's right," Castillo said. "And Steiner don't question how he gets his prisoners. They work the state-owned copper mines and everybody makes a profit and nobody asks any questions about how the inmates are treated or where they come from.

And with a word from me, Steiner would get anything from O'Brien that I want."

"The man would be better off hanging," Old Necessity said.

"My thought exactly," Castillo said bitterly.

"I don't know," Hollis said doubtfully.

"You don't have to," Castillo said in that hard voice. "I made up my mind." He stared past them. "If Steiner don't break him by some chance, the prison will kill him anyway. The hard way."

About mid-afternoon the kangaroo court got under way. The place selected was the saloon and it was jammed with people. Word had gotten around that they were sending O'Brien to Bradenville, and the ones who knew of that terrible place thought that that punishment was a lot more satisfying than hanging.

O'Brien was brought in under heavy guard after the place was already crowded, and there were many insults thrown at him. He was taken over to Old Necessity, who had set up at a rickety table at the far end of the bar. O'Brien's face was bruised badly and he wore a bandage on his left arm. His rawhides were dirty and torn. He stared hard at the old justice of the peace.

"You a circuit judge?" he said harshly.

Old Necessity ignored him. "The case of The People Against O'Brien," he said loudly. "How do you plead, prisoner?"

"What's the charge?" O'Brien said.

Castillo spoke up. "You know the charges. Murder and rape."

There was an angry uproar in the saloon.

"Not guilty," O'Brien answered. There was more noise.

"All right, sheriff," Old Necessity said. "Tell your story."

Castillo stood beside the table, facing the crowd, and the noise subsided. He went through the story of finding O'Brien at the medicine wagon, and about the rifle and the money pouch. "It was clear to all of us that he was one of the killers," he concluded.

Castillo moved away to cheers from the crowd. Old Necessity then called the members of the posse, one by one, and each one verified Castillo's story. Finally they were all finished.

"Now you can tell your side of it," Old Necessity said then to O'Brien, in a sarcastic tone.

O'Brien looked at the hard faces around the room and knew how pointless it all was. "Go to hell," he said in a low growl.

There was another uproar. When the crowd had settled down, Old Necessity cleared his throat. "All right. I sentence you to life imprisonment at hard labor, at the state prison at Bradenville."

For some reason, hearing those words did something to O'Brien. An ugly, primitive sound started in his throat, as his big arms pulled against the ropes that held him and suddenly tore them free.

Before the sheriff or any of the deputized men realized O'Brien was loose, O'Brien had moved to the table that Old Necessity sat behind. O'Brien picked the table up in a sweeping motion, to the gasps and exclamations from the crowd, and turned and hurled it at the sheriff just as he pulled his gun. The table crashed into Castillo and two of his armed men, knocking them all to the floor with the table on top of them. One of the deputies was struck in the head by the hard corner of the table and was killed instantly.

While the three were lying on the floor, and the other two were still gazing stupidly at them, O'Brien picked the old man off his chair and lifted him above his head, Old Necessity's face going white and his eyes bugging out. O'Brien turned and hurled the judge at the other two deputies. Both of them had recovered and had aimed their revolvers at O'Brien, but were unable to fire when the form of the J.P. came hurtling at them. He crashed into them and threw them both back against the mahogany bar, cracking a vertebra in the back of the biggest one. The second man's gun went off and missed O'Brien, splintering the ceiling of hand-rived oak.

"Get him!" a loud, high voice came. It was Mayor Hollis, who had kept in the background until now.

Most of the townspeople had scurried out the swinging doors of the place at the first action. A few of the bigger men remained, unarmed at the sheriff's insistence, and one threw himself now at O'Brien, with a knife in hand.

O'Brien caught the knife hand of the man and simultaneously threw a knee into the man's groin. The man doubled up in pain, and O'Brien twisted the knife out of his hand. When two more men landed suddenly on O'Brien's back, he threw one off, cracking the man's skull on the hardwood floor when he hit, and then O'Brien jammed an elbow into the other one's side, cracking ribs.

At that point, the sheriff and the live deputy

with him had both regained their feet, and even though Castillo had lost his gun, the deputy had not. The deputy aimed at O'Brien.

O'Brien saw the move, and released the knife he had taken from his assailant. It sunk in the deputy's belly, and his gun went off harmlessly into the floor.

While the sheriff found his gun, four more men converged on O'Brien at once, before he saw them coming, and then he was off his feet and slugging at them from the floor. When the remaining men saw him down, they all piled on, beating and pummeling him. In just a few seconds, he was being held by several men and beaten by the rest. And they intended to keep at it until they had killed him.

But then the sheriff found his gun and fired it off at the ceiling, stopping them. "Okay, you got him," he said. "Let's save him for Bradenville."

One by one the men piled off O'Brien, and when the sheriff looked down on the buffalo hunter, O'Brien was only half-conscious, but there was a look of stubborn, unrelenting defiance in his face. O'Brien tried to see the sheriff through half-closed eyes, his face bloody.

"You better kill me now," O'Brien said thickly. "You better—just kill me now, sheriff."

Castillo shook his head slowly, then kicked O'Brien hard in the side. He grinned a tight grin when he saw O'Brien grimace in pain. "You know, hunter," he said tightly, "I'm going to enjoy thinking of you in that hell hole of Steiner's. I'm going to enjoy it a whole lot."

4

The prison compound and the adjacent mine with its hills of slag surrounding it were an open sore on the otherwise green and tawny brown landscape. It was Bradenville State Prison, located just a few miles from a crossroads village by the same name.

There were two compounds, one for the prison proper and the other for the mine operation, and they were separated and surrounded by high barbed wire. There were six guard towers around the place, each equipped with a Gatling gun. There were several low buildings in the prison compound, and a two-storey house where the warden lived. The entire place, except for the house, was infested with lice, rats, and disease, and it was said by those who had been confined there that if a man could last out a year at Bradenville, he would have no difficulty spending eternity in hell.

On the day that O'Brien arrived, the prisoners had just returned from the mine and were being allowed their daily outing in the prison compound. There were over two hundred of them milling about out there, white-faced from fatigue and sickness and mistreatment. Many were lying on the hard dirt, unable to stand after their day in the mine. When the wagon bearing O'Brien pulled up at the main gate to the place, the ones who were able moved over to that area to watch the new prisoner admitted.

There was a short exchange of words between the guard and the two deputies on the wagon, and then the vehicle rumbled into the compound. It was a flat wagon, and Castillo had built a cage and placed it on the wagon to contain O'Brien, to emphasize to those who saw him arrive that they were receiving something less than a man.

The chalky faces with their grimy beards stared unblinking at the cage on the wagon as it moved into the compound and stopped among them. The sun was setting behind a distant hill, giving a strange light to the scene. The gaunt half-men of Bradenville clustered around the cage now, mumbling to each other and poking their fingers toward O'Brien, while a guard went to bring Steiner to greet the newcomer.

O'Brien sat on the bottom of the cage, his long hair wild, a stubble of beard already appearing around the handlebar mustache he always wore. His cold blue eyes narrowed as he slowly took in the scene before him, looking from one ghostly face to the other. So this was Bradenville, he thought.

"Hey, look at that one!" a small prisoner said.

"They taking grizzlies here now?" a big man laughed harshly.

A third prisoner picked up a rock and threw it into the cage and hit O'Brien in the head, making his ear bleed. "Let's see if the bear can perform for us."

O'Brien ducked slightly when the rock came, otherwise made no movement or sound. He felt a nausea welling up inside him, just looking at these men and at the place where they lived and died. O'Brien had never been confined before in his life, except temporarily, and the thought of spending the rest of his days here in this rat hole made him physically sick.

Suddenly all the faces were turned away from him, and were looking toward the clapboard house where warden Steiner lived and had his offices. Steiner was moving down the slope of ground toward the wagon, with another man. In a moment they stood beside the wagon, and were speaking with the deputies Castillo had sent. Steiner was a big man who dressed like an easterner and in fact had served in penal institutions in Massachusetts and Pennsylvania before moving west. He had been discharged from each of the last two prisons where he had served, for brutality and insubordination. Beside him was a rather short man dressed like a Texan and whose name was Quinn. Quinn was Steiner's captain of the guard, called simply "The Man" by the prisoners, and he was a sadist who thrived on the suffering of others.

"So this is O'Brien," Steiner said, standing with his hands clasped behind him. He had received a wire and letter from Castillo, and had been told what Castillo wanted, and warned about O'Brien. Steiner enjoyed nothing more than receiving a new man who had a reputation for being tough. The others were no challenge to him.

Quinn walked over to the cage and peered into it, and O'Brien turned his shaggy head and stared into those psychotic eyes for a long moment, with their mirthless glittering. Quinn ran a riding stick along the wooden pole bars of the cage, watching O'Brien's reaction. "He don't look so special to me, warden," he said in a quiet, hard voice that put a chill down the backs of the prisoners. The man had almost no eyebrows, and the lower part of his face was pock-marked. His hair was dark and O'Brien wondered if there were not some Indian in him. He wore a small gold ring in his left ear, through the lobe.

The prisoners had retreated from the wagon at Steiner's appraoch, cowering away in fear and hatred, and O'Brien noticed now that their faces had ceased to watch him and all, without exception, were turned toward Steiner and Quinn, silent and grim.

"Well, take it from me," a deputy said to Quinn, "he's as mean as they come."

"Good," Steiner grinned, watching the big man in the cage. "That's the kind we like here. All right, you can bring him out of there, guards."

The deputies unlocked the cage, watching O'Brien every moment, and then two prison guards went inside and began dragging O'Brien out of the cage feet first. O'Brien, whose hands were tied in front of him, managed to reach out and grab at one of the wooden bars, checking his slide along the cage floor.

"I'm a man," he said in a low voice. "I can walk. Untie my feet."

A hush settled over the area as they all heard him speak for the first time. Then Quinn reacted first. Standing outside the cage near O'Brien, he took the riding crop and brought it down hard on O'Brien's fingers that had grabbed the bar. O'Brien grunted and released the bar, and Quinn laughed, and was joined by several deputies and guards. The prisoners were still grimly silent, their faces tense.

When the guards began dragging O'Brien again, he kicked out savagely with his bound feet at the closest one, and broke the man's leg and knee-cap. There was a loud murmur rising from the prisoners as the guard yelled aloud and fell out of the cage and to the ground, then lay there writhing in pain. The other one stepped away from O'Brien quickly, pulling his gun, and just missing a second kick from O'Brien.

Steiner was aghast at the development, and anger rose quickly in him. Quinn stood looking at O'Brien with a new look of respect on his face. O'Brien, ignoring the gun on him, kicked out at the second guard again, grazing the man's shin and busting a bar out of the wooden cage. The man lost the gun through the bars that time, and when he found himself without one, jumped headlong out the open cage door to the ground, wrenching his shoulder as he hit. He had been seized with sudden panic when he found himself in there alone with the man in rawhides, without a gun.

Steiner looked down at the second guard on the

ground, with hard eyes, and then back at O'Brien, still bound hand and foot in the cage. Quinn came around to him now, and when he spoke, his voice had a hoarse quality to it.

"I'll get him out of there," he said, his voice trembling with restrained excitement. "Just give me a few guards and I'll get him out of there."

A deputy, gun in hand now, shook his head. "We tried to tell you about him," he said.

Steiner stared at O'Brien another long moment. "Untie his feet," he said.

Quinn looked over at him as if he were crazy, but Steiner put his hand up to forestall an exclamation. "You heard me. Untie his feet," Steiner said.

Quinn grudgingly relayed the order to two other guards. They moved to the cage warily, moving past the two guards who had been attacked. They entered the cage, O'Brien watching them with his hard eyes, and gingerly began to untie O'Brien's feet. In a moment they were loose, and the men quickly retreated out of the cage. There was another murmuring from the prisoners.

Steiner had already lost face before the prisoners and guards, and to prolong getting O'Brien out of the cage would have made it even worse, and he knew it. Once O'Brien was off the wagon, Steiner would make things right.

"All right, now come out of there," Steiner said to O'Brien.

Over two hundred faces turned to O'Brien as he struggled to his feet inside the cage, crouched through its door, and jumped to the ground. There was a rustle of whispering voices as they saw the size of him. Steiner stood just a few feet from

O'Brien, with Quinn beside him. Quinn unconsciously stepped back a pace.

"You haven't been here a half hour," Steiner said, "and you've caused trouble." He glanced at the maimed guard on the ground, and at the other one who had gotten to his feet, holding his shoulder. "Well, we got ways of handling troublemakers at Bradenville. Guards."

A half dozen guards, armed with rifles and revolvers, now came and formed a half-circle around O'Brien, with his back to the wagon. Steiner and Quinn retreated out of the circle, and Steiner took a long black whip from a guard.

"Quinn, I'd like you to give this man twenty lashes. Personally."

Quinn looked at Steiner with a small grin, and accepted the whip. He stepped into the circle, confident with the guards all around him. The prisoners stood grim-faced.

"With pleasure," Quinn said.

He made no effort to get O'Brien's ripped rawhide shirt off first. It made little difference, anyway. Twenty lashes would cut him up good. He lashed out with the whip viciously, and O'Brien ducked his head and it struck him across the head and chest, laying open a gash over a foot long. O'Brien felt the sting of it and moved the bruised fingers of his hands and hated the smirk on the short man's face as he brought the whip forward again.

The scene was grimly silent, except for the cracking of the horsehide whip on O'Brien's body. On the fourth time, backed against the wagon, O'Brien had had enough of it. He had decided to wait it out, but it was not in his nature to do so. He caught the whip in his bound hands before Quinn could bring it back to him, and then pulled savagely on it. Quinn was taken by surprise and could not let go in time. He was pulled violently toward O'Brien, stumbling to keep his balance. When he reached O'Brien, O'Brien swung his big hands down onto the back of Quinn's head, smashing the man down against the wagon and then to the ground.

O'Brien then threw himself at Steiner, several paces away. O'Brien knocked two guards down to get to Steiner, and was at that man's throat with his hands, choking off Steiner's breath and turning his face blue, when the guards recovered and ganged up on O'Brien from behind. O'Brien felt the first two hits with the gun barrels, and then fell to the ground as the guards literally beat him senseless with their weapons.

Steiner, who had sagged to his knees, now was on his feet again, gasping for air and holding his throat. "Don't—kill him," he choked. "Save him for—the hot box."

And that was what they did. Even before the deputies who brought O'Brien had left, the prison guards had stripped O'Brien's battered body bare of all clothing and had dragged him across the compound to one of three metal boxes which were built off the ground on three-foot poles. The boxes were built just big enough to put a man in, if he did not try to rise from a sitting position. There was one opening, the metal door on the front of the box, where they put the prisoner in and took him out. The boxes were situated so that they stood in the broiling sun all through the day, and some of the prisoners refered to them as furnaces.

Now, as dusk settled over the compound, Steiner and Quinn watched with dark and saturnine faces as two guards dumped O'Brien's unconscious, naked form into the box.

"We'll start out with a little solitary confinement," Steiner said, using a mild penal term for the boxes, "and then work up from there." He felt the bruises on his throat.

Quinn stood unsteadily beside him. He felt as if he had been caught in a mine explosion. "Yeah," he said. "A couple weeks in the hot box ought to soften him up real nice."

The guard swung the iron door closed and slapped a heavy padlock closed on it. Then the guard, at Steiner's command, opened the box next to the one O'Brien was in. When the door swung open, a limp form fell out onto the ground. The bony figure had sores and wounds all over it, and there were maggots crawling in them. The man was very dead, the eyes open in pain now gone.

"Looks like we left Johnson in there a mite too long," Steiner said.

The guard dragged the body off, while Steiner and Quinn walked together to the clapboard dwelling at the rear of the compound.

O'Brien did not come to until the middle of the night. At first he had no idea where he was or how he had gotten there, but as he lay there focusing his brain, it slowly came back to him. Looking around the small enclosure, he knew what they had done to him, because he had seen the boxes from the cage. Moonlight slithered through a couple of cracks where the metal came together, and O'Brien found himself wondering just how bad it would get when the sun was directly overhead the next day. The place stunk of feces and urine and something else he could not identify. Lying there propped on an elbow, he felt a presence in the box with him, and a moment later he found out what it was when a big rat ran over his leg and made a dash for a rusty hole in the back corner of the box. O'Brien made no move to kill it. He did not have it in him. He felt like his head would split wide open if he moved at all, so he just lay there, waiting to fall off again.

O'Brien's next two weeks were hell. If a man went into the hot box healthy, it could kill him, and O'Brien was not healthy. The first afternoon, he thought he would die fast—either suffocate or burn up, but somehow the sun went down and the night came and he survived. After the second day he learned to lie on his side in the afternoon with his head to the rat hole, sucking air in from that small aperture, and trying not to think about his flesh burning against the hot metal.

Nobody came to open the box for several days, and by that time he was suffering badly from thirst, and the box was accumulating his own waste, and it was difficult not to lie in it. Finally, one day he heard a clanging outside the door, and it miraculously opened. A big guard stood there, but O'Brien could see only his silhouette, his eyes unused to the light. The man laughed at him.

"I suppose you want some water?" the voice came. "Well, have some." Before O'Brien knew what he was doing, the guard took a full cup of water and poured it onto the dirty floor of the hot box. With another derisive laugh, the man slammed the door closed again, and O'Brien was again alone.

O'Brien looked at the water standing on the floor of the cubicle, and he looked back at the locked door. Suddenly a cry rose from his throat, and burst forth like a roar. "Damn you!" he yelled, beating with his fists on the door. "Damn you!"

Then, later, he got down on all fours and drank the putrid stinking water from the floor, like an animal. It was a matter of drinking it, or dying.

In the next several days, before the water came again, O'Brien thought he would go mad. It was not the thirst, nor hunger, nor the awful pain that wracked his cramped, battered body. It was not even the awful baking he endured every afternoon, nor the threat of suffocation. It was the four walls of the tiny cubicle, the awful feeling of confinement so heightened as to become an obsession in his fevered brain. On the day before the water came again, he went quite mad for a couple of hours, and vainly tried to kick and scratch his way through the metal walls, making his hands bleed badly and bruising himself all over again, making animal noises in his throat all the while. When he finally gave up, he fell into a fitful sleep and had a nightmare about Comanches and being roasted alive over a fire.

When the water was brought the second time, O'Brien squatted in the far corner of the hot box and watched silently with slitted eyes and wished the man was not holding a gun. This man did not dump the water, however. He set a tin cup of it inside and left it, then locked the door again. O'Brien could not believe it. He approached the cup warily, as if it might explode in his face somehow. He sniffed at it, and there was no doubt of it. It was fresh water. O'Brien picked the cup up carefully, and let the cool wetness run into his mouth. That night, he slept well.

O'Brien had been in the place almost a week when that second water came, and still they had not fed him. It was clear that Steiner intended to weaken him with hunger and privation, and have O'Brien come out, if ever, a very humble prisoner. Maybe Steiner was not going to let him out, he thought over and over again. Maybe he wanted him to die in here, a little at a time.

On the day after the second water, O'Brien decided he had to adjust to survive. He had to quit hitting out blindly, and be clever. That afternoon he found a scorpion in the box with him, and instead of looking on it as a danger, he saw it as a bounty. He killed it carefully, pulled the tail off, and ate it. It made him nauseous, but he kept it down. The next day a lizard wandered in and he cornered it, and had a better meal. But he was still getting weaker and weaker. The following night he got lucky. The rat wandered in again. O'Brien lay quietly as if he were asleep, until he could be sure he could cut the rat off from escape. Then he blocked the hole it entered by with his foot, and trapped the animal. He got a small gash on his hand before he wrung its neck. Then he skinned it and disembowelled it and ate it. The hunger pangs in his stomach lessened for the first time in days.

When the next water came, the man threw in a couple of pieces of dirty hardtack, and O'Brien clutched it to his big chest and retreated to a corner while a second man cleaned the floor of the box for the first time. O'Brien hoarded the bread, and was glad he did, because he got no more for the rest of his time in the box, which was almost another week. During that time he killed two more lizards to supplement the bread, and although his weight went down considerably during the box time, when they finally opened the door for his personal exit, he was reasonably alert and vital. Steiner himself came to see O'Brien emerge, along with Quinn and a guard they called Purvis, a big, scraggly-haired man with a receded chin.

"All right, hunter," Steiner called in to O'Brien. "You can come out if you've learned to behave."

O'Brien had become cunning in the box. He did not want them to know he had preserved some strength, so he did not show it. He crawled from the box on his elbows and dropped to the ground at their feet. Then he lay there letting the muscles in his legs uncramp. He could not have walked if his life depended on it, or even stood erect.

"Well," Quinn said in his smooth ugly voice. "That's a different man from the one we put in there. You sure we got the right box?"

Steiner chuckled at the small joke, and looked O'Brien over. His naked body was dirt-smeared and crusty with scabs and burns from the oven they had kept him in. His beard was almost as long as his mustache now, and he looked gaunt under it. There were lice crawling in his hair. And he stunk worse than he ever had on the buffalo trail.

"Well, are you ready to apologize for the way you acted when they brought you in here?" Steiner said. He was surrounded by three guards in addition to Quinn. "Or would you rather spend another couple of weeks in the hot box?"

O'Brien, although he could have answered him, did not. He let his head hang toward the ground weakly. Quinn moved over to him and kicked O'Brien onto his side, and O'Brien looked up into that pockmarked face and remembered the nights he had lain in that box and seen it and hated it. The list seemed to grow, and he had to divide his hatred between these two and Castillo and Latimer who had caused the whole thing. But he had plenty of it to divide.

"Well?" Quinn said tautly. "Can't you talk, prisoner?"

O'Brien moved his mouth. "Yeah," he said.

"Then, talk," Steiner said.

"I'm sorry—for what—happened."

Steiner grinned widely. He looked around at the faces of the guards and they grinned back at him. "Well, now. Isn't that nice?" Steiner said. "You boys have just witnessed a grizzly bear turn into a lamb before your very eyes."

A couple of them laughed. O'Brien lay there and flexed his leg muscles and tried not to listen to the laughing. There was a way to survive this, there had to be. And it had to do with holding the anger inside and being clever. So O'Brien would try, for a while, to be clever.

"Take him to the barracks and let him bathe," Steiner said to the guards. "Then find a cell for him. Tomorrow morning he goes down into the mine with the others."

O'Brien struggled to his knees, and then to his feet. He thought that, if he were careful, he might be able to walk. Watching Steiner and Quinn move away from him across the compound, he knew that, after the obsession with his personal freedom, his hatred for these two men would help in sustaining him in his fight for survival. His hatred for them, and for Castillo and Reuben Latimer. Latimer whose place he was taking in this Godforsaken place. No, he would not forget Latimer.

5

The Latimer gang picketed their mounts quietly outside the Hodgenville Bank, raising a fine dust in the early morning sun. There were five men now, because Latimer had picked up two gunfighters in the past week. One was called Sidewinder, a tall, gaunt fellow known for back-shooting, and the other was a quiet sidekick of his named Waco. They were wanted in four states. They had brought news to Latimer of O'Brien's arrest and imprisonment, and they had all had a good laugh over the mix-up the law had made, and decided to celebrate it by robbing the Hodgenville Bank.

The street was empty. Without speaking, Reuben pulled his bandana up over his face and the others did likewise. Then they stepped into the bank. A woman, one of four customers inside, saw them and cried out.

"Don't do that again, lady," Ayers told her quietly.

"This is a stick-up," Reuben announced loudly. "Stay where you are!"

A man suddenly came in behind them. He took one look and tried to run back out, his face panic-stricken. Ayers grinned and shot him in the back as he moved out the door, and the man hit the walk just outside the door, clutching at his back. Sidewinder fired another shot into the man and the fellow jerked spasmodically and lay still.

Reuben stuck a white cloth bag at the nearest teller. "All right, fill that up!" he said.

The woman who had made the outcry earlier now fainted away and fell to the floor. The three men backed away from the robbers, watching them silently. Only one of them was armed.

"Don't kill us!" one of the unarmed men said.

Sarge stood near the door and watched for the marshal while the teller fumbled with the bag.

"Hurry it up!" Reuben said loudly.

"I only got small bills here," the teller apologized.

Just then the door to a small office opened, and the bank president stood in the doorway. He took one look at what was happening, and drew the gun on his hip in panic. Waco turned his Colt on him and fired and hit the banker in the chest, knocking him back through the door.

The other teller also panicked then, and started toward the door the banker had just emerged from. Reuben shot him down before he had taken two steps, then coldly shot him again as he hit the floor.

The other teller and the men customers looked bug-eyed.

"You want to try that?" Reuben asked the teller.

"I ain't one to argue with artillery," the man said weakly.

"Then move your freight," Reuben warned him.

"We got to get out of here," Sarge said from the door.

While the teller worked feverishly to fill the bag, the woman came to and sat up groggily. Taking another look at her, Ayers went over and pulled a necklace off her neck and examined it. She gasped again, and struggled to her feet.

"That's a family heirloom!" she said weakly. She went to Ayers and tried to grab the necklace back, and he held it out of her grasp.

"Now ain't that too bad," Ayers said, grinning. He grabbed the woman and pulled her to him, running his hands over her and kissing her hard on the lips. After a moment she pulled away, terrified.

"You animal!" she yelled at him.

Reuben glanced over at Ayers, and saw Waco shaking his head slowly. "Leave her alone, Ayers," Reuben said. "We come for gold."

"Sure, Reuben," Ayers said, grinning at the woman and looking down then at the necklace. He stuffed it into a pocket.

The teller was now hefting the bag out through the window to Reuben, full of coins and paper money. Reuben grabbed it and hefted it. "There better be some real money in here," he said to the teller.

"Somebody stop them!" the woman said hysterically. She turned to the man with the gun on his hip. "You have a gun! What's the matter with you?"

Reuben slapped the woman hard in the face and knocked her to the floor, silencing her. Then he looked at the others. "Let's get out of here," he said.

The five of them moved back out the way they had come then, Sarge and Sidewinder last. Just as those last two turned away from him, the customer with the gun played the hero for a moment and pulled his gun to get them as they left. But Sidewinder heard the movement and turned before the man could clear his holster. Sidewinder blasted the customer in the face, and crimson exploded over it. The man slammed against the wall behind him, leaving a large red splotch there before he hit the floor.

Outside, they were just ready to mount, when Sarge yelled, "There's the law!"

They looked down the street, and the marshal and a deputy stood blocking their way with rifles. "Hold it right there, boys!" the lawman yelled at them.

The robbers answered by opening fire on them. There was a loud, wild exchange, filling the small street with gunsmoke. Sarge was hit in the shoulder with a rifle slug immediately, and fell. Ayers' cavalry cap was ripped off his head and forever lost. The marshal himself was hit twice before he could reach cover, once in the hip and then in the side. He fell in the street and could not make cover.

The deputy had dived behind a trough across the street without being hit. The robbers ducked behind their mounts and whatever other cover they could find, firing back wildly.

"Get the deputy!" Reuben was yelling, crouched on the walk grasping the bag of money tightly.

The marshal had lost his weapon and was semi-conscious, out of the fight, and nobody paid any further attention to him. But the deputy was firing from the trough, pinning them down. He hit Ayers' mount, and dropped it, and the animal kicked violently as it fell onto its side in the street. Reuben and Waco dived behind it.

"Get that man, damn it!" Reuben said again.

Sidewinder nodded his head, and disappeared around the side of the bank building, while the others continued to return fire to the deputy.

"You might as well come out of there," Reuben called to the man. "We're going to kill you if you don't."

"You drop that gold and leave, and I will," the deputy yelled back at him.

"I'm having a little trouble hearing you, when you talk like that," Reuben called to him.

"Why don't you just drop the gold and leave," the spunky lawman insisted.

"It's a mite too late for that," Reuben told him. "Now you come on out of there, and we'll tie you up and let you out of this with your hide. If not, we're going to have to shoot you."

There was a sielnce from the water trough.

"Get over by Sarge's mount," Reuben said to Ayers. "And be ready to help him aboard it when the time comes."

"You just leave the gold," the deputy finally said again. Reuben and his men answered by firing a volley at the trough, putting more holes in it and causing the water to spout out its sides in narrow ribbons. The deputy raised up briefly and returned their fire, and just missed Reuben's head, making him swear under his breath.

But then the four of them could all see Sidewinder appear from the corner of a building behind the deputy, with a big grin on his face. The treacherous back-shooter had removed his boots and was now creeping up on the deputy from behind noiselessly.

"You better give it up, deputy," Reuben said, keeping the man's attention on them.

"Yeah," Ayers called out, "this is your last chance, lawman. Your last chance for your life."

"Just leave the gold, and—"

Those were the last words the deputy would ever utter. He heard a small sound in back of him and turned to see the grinning face of Sidewinder. Sidewinder shot him through the back, before the deputy could turn his body to face him. The deputy dropped the rifle and fell over the tank, then staggered away from it into the middle of the street, clutching his torso. The robbers took that opportunity to make sure of him. Reuben and Ayers both fired twice at him, three slugs hitting the deputy before his limp form struck the dirt underfoot, jerking him around in the street like a grisly puppet on a string. When the firing ended, the deputy's body was a bloody mess.

Reuben then walked over to the marshal, aimed his gun at the man's chest, and pulled off another round into him. The marshal quivered and expired. Reuben turned to the others.

"Mount up!" he said.

They helped Sarge onto his mount behind Ayers, and then they rode back down the dirt street, thundering away in a great fog of dust. With the bag of money secure on Reuben's mount, the Latimer gang was in business.

O'Brien had been allowed to wash off when he was released from the solitary confinement box, and then was given a set of gray dungarees that matched those of the other prisoners, and his boots were returned to him. "You won't ever be needing the other stuff again," the guard Purvis had said to him, grinning. O'Brien was then taken to a barracks, which was a lice-infested rat hole, and thrown into a wire cage in there with three other prisoners. The place was divided into ten cages or cells, four prisoners to a cell, and an aisleway between them.

The first night O'Brien met his three cell-mates. The guard Purvis gave O'Brien a shove into the cage and O'Brien hit the floor among the other three, who glared at him. Then the cage door was locked and Purvis was gone. O'Brien turned from the guard's retreating back, looked around at the three dehumanized faces, and spoke to them in a low, firm voice.

"How do we get out of this place?" he said.

The three just sat and watched him at a distance. Two of them were ordinary-sized men, and the third one was a big one, about O'Brien's size. The big one looked better-fed and healthier than the others.

"Can't any of you talk?" O'Brien said to them. "Or have you forgot how?"

They squatted and sat on the wood floor around him in the semi-darkness of dusk and watched him silently. O'Brien looked again from one face to the next, trying to see behind their eyes. Finally he gave it up and went and sat in a corner that was unoccupied.

"All right, to hell with you," he said, not looking at any of them.

One of the two smaller men leaned forward toward O'Brien. He was a wiry fellow with balding hair and an intelligent, serious face. "My name's Brady," he said.

O'Brien regarded him coolly. "All right, Brady," he said.

The big man suddenly spoke up loudly. "And I'm Short Hitch, and I own this cage," he said. He glowered at O'Brien menacingly.

"Own it?" O'Brien said to him.

Brady answered for the big man. "Every cage has its pecking order. Short Hitch is biggest, so he's what we call the baron of this here cage. Then comes me, because I'm faster and smarter than The Owl." Brady jerked a thumb at the third man, a very gaunt, pasty-faced individual wearing steel-rimmed glasses.

"I'm The Owl," the man said to O'Brien. "I can see in the dark."

"That's the truth," Brady acknowledged. "And he has ways of finding out things before the rest of us. He always gets the rumors first around here."

A man from an adjoining cell called over. "And it's usually wrong information, too."

The Owl turned sullenly. "Dry up," he commented.

"It's the smallest and weakest men," Brady continued, "and newcomers that end up at the bottom of the list in a cage." He had stressed the word 'newcomers' when he came to it, looking pointedly at O'Brien.

"Nice system," O'Brien said.

"*You* don't have to like it," Short Hitch said.

O'Brien grunted. He would not make an issue of anything tonight. He needed rest badly. He needed to heal.

"There are some things you ought to know," Brady continued, "if you figure on making it through your first full day here. One is, avoid Purvis."

"That's the guard that brought me?"

"That's right. He hasn't got it all up here." He pointed to his head. "And he's a mean one. I guess you've already met Steiner and Quinn."

O'Brien looked at him. "Yeah," he said.

"Well, butter them up, or you're a dead man."

"I'll keep that in mind."

"They'll send you down below tomorrow," The Owl said.

"Below?" O'Brien said.

"Into the mine," Brady said. "They'll be watching you like a hawk your first day, so you better make a good impression. If you so much as scratch your ear, you have to get permission from The Man."

"Quinn?"

"That's him. He just loves to show a new man who's running the place," Brady said. "So keep a low profile and keep digging."

"Why are you telling me all this?" O'Brien asked.

Brady looked at him with his cold eyes. "Because you're another back to help keep ours from breaking," he said. "And it would be a shame to lose you before we get any work out of you."

O'Brien grunted.

"And one last thing. You asked how to get out of here. The answer is, you don't. Nobody gets out of Bradenville. Some just live longer than others while they're here."

O'Brien looked into Brady's eyes and assimilated that remark. Before he could make a reply, he heard a sound, and it was Purvis again. He came and opened the door of the cage next to theirs, and pointed a finger at a man.

"Brown. Come with me."

A slight man in a far corner of the cell looked with terror at the guard. "It wasn't me, Purvis! I don't know nothing about it!"

"Move, Brown," the big Purvis said, in his heavy twang.

Brown left with Purvis then, and Purvis' lantern

swung out of the building, and the place was now dark.

Brady turned to O'Brien. "A couple sticks of dynamite is missing, and some stoolie put the finger on Brown. Not for taking it, but for knowing who did."

"Dynamite?" O'Brien said.

"We use it in the mine. They guard it like it was gold. Brown will have hell to pay before this night's over."

"What will they do with him?" O'Brien said.

There was a silence from Brady's corner. "Best not to think about that."

O'Brien sat there thinking about it. This was some place that Reuben Latimer and Castillo had gotten him into. He looked over at the silhouette of Brady. "Steiner's got spies among us, then?"

"That's right," The Owl answered for him. "When we find out who they are, they have an accident. It's usually fatal."

The big Short Hitch grunted. "Almost always," he said. He got up and walked over to Brady, and suddenly kicked him in the thigh. Brady let out a muffled cry. "You talk too much to newcomers," he said.

Brady rubbed his leg in the darkness. "Sorry, Short Hitch."

"Now the talking is over," Short Hitch told them. "It's time to get some shut-eye." He moved over to O'Brien, and kicked him in the leg harder than he had Brady, and O'Brien felt the pain shoot through his leg. He looked up angrily, and started to respond, then remembered his weakened condition. He sat there unmoving, silent.

"I'm sleeping in that corner tonight," Short Hitch said to him. "Get away."

O'Brien looked up at the big bulk of the man and remembered his resolution to be clever. He moved away, saying nothing. The corner he moved to stunk of urine, and he tried to ignore it. Both Brady and The Owl had moved to the corner vacated by Short Hitch, and met there in the darkness. The Owl glared at Brady darkly, and Brady smashed a fist into The Owl's face, knocking him down and throwing his glasses off. Brady then sat down in the corner, while The Owl scrambled for his glasses, recovered them grumbling, and retreated to the corner he had left. No one spoke aloud after Short Hitch commanded them not to.

O'Brien tried to find a comfortable position on the wood floor, but could not. He lay there for a long time awake, and finally began hearing distant screams from another part of the camp. That would be Brown. O'Brien listened to the screams punctuate the night for what must have been an hour, then the camp was quiet again. Only then did O'Brien find sleep.

When dawn came, the guards came with it, rousting the prisoners for their daily stint in the bowels of the earth. O'Brien began to understand why these men were so pale, in addition to their mistreatment. They saw very little sun.

There was no morning meal or even coffee. The prisoners were lined up outside their individual barracks and then marched to the mine. When they got there, most went down into the mine to dig out copper ore with picks and shovels all day, with a short break around noon.

Quinn, "The Man", personally oversaw all work that went on at the mine, dividing his time between the shafts themselves and the surface operations. He had guards who assisted in this task, but he was the one the prisoners feared. When Quinn saw O'Brien in the line-up heading down into the dim shaft, he grinned an evil grin but did not speak to O'Brien.

When O'Brien got down to the area they were working in, he was given a pick and told to commence with the rest of them. There were kerosene lanterns set around the shaft for light. O'Brien was put to work near The Owl, and that man gave him a few words of advice.

"Keep your head down and the pick going," he whispered. "And no talking."

O'Brien picked away at the vein of ore with the rest of them all morning, lasting it out although he was very weak. When a man wanted to remove a shirt or even wipe his brow, he would turn to Quinn or a guard, and ask permission. "Take my shirt off, Boss." "Fix my bandana, Boss." "Wipe the sweat off, Boss." The guard would nod, and only then would the prisoner safely cease his work for even a moment. The very worst slave plantations of the South could not have been so bad, O'Brien thought as he worked, so destructive of human dignity. As the morning passed, O'Brien stayed with it, despite his weak condition. And he thought of the Great Plains, and the fresh air and sun on his back, and the hunt, and he knew that he could never adapt to this. He would rather be dead.

At the noon break there was still no food, and O'Brien found that there was only one meal per day, and that was served in the cell when the day was over for them. Water came to them once in the morning, and once in the afternoon. When the afternoon was half over, O'Brien began weakening, and slowing down. He felt near collapse at one point. This attracted the attention of Quinn.

"Well, O'Brien. Did you decide to quit early?" Quinn's smooth voice came to O'Brien, as he paused for a moment in the digging.

O'Brien looked up at him. "I'm— wearing out," he said.

"You didn't request permission to rest," Quinn said. "And if you had, you wouldn't have got it."

The other prisoners near O'Brien turned dirt-smudged faces toward the conversation, but kept picking away at the side of the shaft.

"I need food to work," O'Brien said.

"Oh?" Quinn said, raising his eyebrows. "You want special privileges now, huh? Maybe you want somebody else's ration?"

"No," O'Brien said quickly, looking at the other faces. "I didn't say that."

Quinn grinned a hard grin, and motioned to three guards who had moved over to them. They converged on O'Brien, each with a short club in his hand. The biggest guard brought the club down toward O'Brien. O'Brien put his arm up in defense, but the club still got him across the neck and shoulders, knocking him down to the dirt floor of the shaft near another prisoner, an older man. O'Brien lay there shaking his head from the blow, and then glared up at the three guards, who were working their way in on him.

A voice came whispering into O'Brien's ear from

the prisoner. "Don't fight back!" the man whispered harshly to him. "Whatever they do to you, don't fight back."

The other two guards had reached him now, and almost together they brought their clubs down onto O'Brien. One got him on the shoulder again, and the other hit him alongside the head. He fell back, stunned. The three then bent over him, hitting with the clubs at his head and body. They were careful not to knock him out completely, because there would have been some mercy in that. So O'Brien lay there and did not fight back and was clever. It was not easy. They gave him a real beating, one that would set him back again, and every fiber of his being cried out to hit back, to defend himself. But he lay there and took it, and, finally, it was over.

O'Brien was bruised and bleeding. He lay there breathless from the beating, not looking up at them. He could not look at them without exploding inside. One of them laughed.

"Well," Quinn said to him. "That give you any second thoughts about things?" He waited for a reply.

O'Brien swallowed hard. "Yeah," he said.

"Good. Then get back to work."

O'Brien struggled to his knees, and then his feet, and fell back down. The guards laughed loudly. The prisoners were watching tensely as O'Brien tried again. On the second try, he stayed on his feet. He found his pick and retrieved it.

"Now go to it," a guard said.

O'Brien grasped the pick and knew that in one swing of it he could impale Quinn's ugly head to the wall of the shaft with it. His knuckles tightened over the handle, and he fought something in his chest for a moment. Then he turned and buried the pick into the wall of ore near him, staggering from the effort.

"That's it," Quinn told him. "Now keep at it, prisoner. And if we hear of any more complaints, you're in trouble."

Quinn left then and so did the guards except one, who stayed nearby to oversee the area. O'Brien gritted his teeth and continued picking away slowly, it seeming that each blow would leave him with no more strength to keep at it. But somehow he did, and the afternoon passed, and he completed his first day in the mine.

Back in the cell that evening, O'Brien got his first meal outside the hot box. The guards came and dumped a wooden bowl of scrap meat chunks and pieces of hardtack into each cell, for the prisoners to split as they saw fit.

When O'Brien reached for the bowl, a big foot swung toward him and kicked him in the face. O'Brien was knocked onto his back, where he stared up at Short Hitch incredulously.

"Like I said, I own this cell," Short Hitch said to O'Brien, his dark eyes psychotic in the fading light.

Short Hitch dug into the bowl, eyeing O'Brien occasionally, and took over half the meat and bread. He carried it over to his favorite corner then, and sat there eating, while Brady, watching O'Brien carefully, went and took another portion from the bowl. When he was through with it, The Owl moved to it morosely and took the last piece of meat and two pieces of bread.

O'Brien got the idea quickly. Within this cell, the four of them made their own laws and rules, and they were primitive in the extreme. The guards paid no attention to how they behaved toward each other, once they were locked up for the night. O'Brien crawled to the bowl, looked inside and found one hard piece of bread. He took it out and looked at it. It was not enough.

O'Brien looked at the others, busily eating, as were the prisoners in adjoining cells. In his condition, he could not even tackle Brady. It had to be The Owl. O'Brien laid his bread down and crawled on his knees toward the other man.

When The Owl saw him coming, he clutched his meat to him and glared hostilely at O'Brien. He made no effort to speak to O'Brien. There was nothing to say. O'Brien moved close to him, and when he was within range, threw a fist at The Owl with what strength he had left. The blow caught The Owl on the side of the head and threw him back against the wall. The meat was dropped in the process. O'Brien grabbed quickly at one of the two pieces of meat, and took another chunk of hardtack. The Owl started to try to get the meat back, but O'Brien's eyes stopped him. O'Brien moved back to his corner, and began eating. He ate slowly, so it would stay down.

Through the entire encounter with The Owl, neither Short Hitch nor Brady had taken any particular interest in what was happening, but kept on eating. Later, Purvis came and got the bowls.

When Purvis was gone again, Short Hitch belched loudly, walked over to O'Brien's corner, and urinated beside O'Brien. O'Brien moved away from it and held his temper and said nothing.

The next few days passed a little better for O'Brien. He kept out of trouble with Quinn in the mine, and got a small amount of food each night, and slowly healed, regaining his strength. It was his sixth day in the cage when he challenged Short Hitch's domination of their small four-man society.

The guard dumped the bowl into the cage as usual, and as usual, Short Hitch moved toward it and knelt over it. Then he suddenly looked up into the face of O'Brien. O'Brien's cuts and bruises were healing, and he looked different today to Short Hitch. Short Hitch did not mistake the look in O'Brien's eye.

"Get back till I got mine, or I'll kill you," the wild-eyed big man told O'Brien.

O'Brien circled the bowl as Short Hitch stood. "Then kill me," O'Brien said.

The other man's eyes slitted down, and he squared off with O'Brien. Brady and The Owl kept in their corners and watched with considerable interest. Men in the other cells chewed at their horse meat and eyed the two big men.

O'Brien moved the bowl toward Brady with his foot. "Don't touch it till we're through," he said. Brady picked up the bowl and got it out of harm's way. Then it began.

Short Hitch slammed a heavy fist into O'Brien's face, and O'Brien only partially blocked the blow. While O'Brien was recovering, the other man drove a knee into O'Brien's groin, doubling him up, and then rammed another fist into O'Brien's head, knocking him to the floor.

The barracks had fallen very quiet, and the sounds of the men fighting were the only sounds in the building. Short Hitch moved over to kick out at O'Brien, and O'Brien grabbed the other man's foot and pulled. Short Hitch lost his balance and slammed heavily to the floor. While he recovered, O'Brien had time to regain his feet. When Short Hitch raised up from the floor, grunting, O'Brien met him with a short uppercut to the face with his left hand, and then smashed a right fist into the side of the other man's head. Short Hitch grunted loudly, and slammed against the wire of the cage, bulging it and cracking a support plank.

Short Hitch got a new look in his eyes as he sagged against the wire. He was going to finish O'Brien off now, and waste no time about it. "I'm going to chew you up and spit you out on the floor of this cage," he said.

He lunged at O'Brien then, and the weight of him threw O'Brien off his feet again and they hit the floor with Short Hitch on top of O'Brien. In an instant Short Hitch was at O'Brien's throat, and he was trying very hard to strangle O'Brien. His big fingers closed hard on O'Brien's throat, and O'Brien did not seem to have the strength to force the hands off him. In a short moment, O'Brien was not getting enough air to breathe, and he knew he did not have long. He let go of the other man's hands then, letting them dig deeper into his windpipe, and began pummeling the other man. He crashed a fist hard into Short Hitch's head and face, with the strength of a dying man. His breath was getting shallower, and his face was turning color, and he had begun gasping for breath. But still he jammed the fist into the big man's head and face, making blood run down the side of it. Short Hitch grunted under the fourth punch, and his grip loosened just slightly on O'Brien's throat. O'Brien gathered all his remaining strength, and viciously struck the head again, and heard the jawbone snap.

Short Hitch yelled a garbled yell and released his hold on O'Brien just momentarily. O'Brien grasped the small advantage and pushed the big man away from him, then got a foot against his groin. O'Brien shoved hard, and Short Hitch went flying off O'Brien and against the back wall of the cell.

O'Brien, gasping for air, struggled to his feet just as Short Hitch came off the wall at him again. O'Brien wearily realized he could not last much longer. As the bull of a man came at him in a wild lunge, O'Brien this time took a step to one side as the other man reached him with his grasping hams of hands, and Short Hitch missed O'Brien. In back of O'Brien was the line of iron bars that ran the length of the building on either side of the aisle, and which formed the front wall of each cage. O'Brien grabbed Short Hitch as he stumbled past, and with all the strength he had, shoved the big man toward the bars violently, driving him into them with O'Brien's full weight behind the man. Short Hitch jammed up against the bars head-first, and the crash shook the building. His head glanced off one bar and drove tightly between it and the next one, cracking his skull on both sides and wedging his head between the bars.

Short Hitch hung there a moment, eyes bugged out, blood spurting from either side of his head, and then the weight of his body pulled his smashed face and head from the bars, leaving bits of flesh stuck there, and he slid to the floor of the cage.

O'Brien walked over to him and kicked the still form and saw that Short Hitch was dead. Brady and The Owl stared wide-eyed at the new corpse on the floor, and in the other cages, prisoners had stopped eating to see what O'Brien had done.

O'Brien looked up from the dead prisoner and around at the silent faces. He turned to Brady. "Now divide that stuff up three ways," he said. "Equally."

Brady looked up at him with a new respect in his eyes. "Anything you say, O'Brien," he said.

As Brady was splitting the grub, Purvis walked in and saw the body of Short Hitch on the floor. "Who done that?" he said.

O'Brien regarded the guard with hard eyes. "Me," he said to him.

Purvis rubbed his chinless face and scowled at O'Brien. Then a grin came onto his crooked mouth as he saw the blood. He grunted. "Well. That's a purty mess." He unlocked the door of the cage. "Okay, you. You killed him. Now you drag him outside and bury him. That's the rules."

O'Brien looked from the guard to the corpse. So that was the punishment for killing another member of your group. You had to bury the body. He shook his head, bent over and grabbed the feet of the dead man, and turned briefly to Brady. "There better be a third of that grub left when I get back," he said. Then he dragged the body from the cell.

7

"I just heard something about you," Brady said to O'Brien.

O'Brien was leaning up against the tangled-barbed-wire fence that surrounded the prison compound, watching the sun set in a fiery ball behind a distant hill. The exercise period was just about over, and soon they would all be back in the stinking cells, and O'Brien had wanted to be alone. But Brady had found him.

"Yeah?" O'Brien said, not looking at Brady. With the slow passage of two more weeks, O'Brien was looking and feeling like a different man, although he knew he would never recover full strength here.

"The grapevine has it that you were part of that Sandy Creek massacre."

O'Brien appraised the other man coolly. "Is that right?"

"That's the word. And that you were with Reuben Latimer, and were part of his gang."

"Don't believe everything you hear," O'Brien told him.

Brady grinned. "I don't. But you seem like Reuben's type. He always surrounded himself with tough ones."

O'Brien turned to look into Brady's face. "You talk like you know the man."

Brady was still grinning. "Didn't old Reuben ever mention me? I rode with him in the old days, down by the border."

O'Brien's brain began working. "He never mentioned you."

Brady grunted. "I heard something else, too, O'Brien. The word is that Steiner is supposed to make you talk."

"Talk?" O'Brien said.

"They think you know where Latimer is. If you do, you'd better tell them. They got ways of working on a man."

"I know. But Reuben didn't tell me where he was headed."

Brady glanced at him. "Which way did he ride out?"

"South," O'Brien said, remembering.

"South? Why, I know where that mangy mustang is headed," Brady exclaimed. "To Villa Bella," he said softly, dropping his voice. "It's a town just over the Mexican border. Reuben used to hole up in a little place of his outside of town, when things got hot in Texas."

O'Brien looked at him. "You been there?"

"Just once. But I could lead you right to it. Look, if they make you talk— don't mention me."

"I won't spill my guts about it," O Brien said. "You see, Brady, I'm going to rejoin the gang."

"Re-join—?"

O'Brien regarded him with burning eyes. Yes, he would plan his escape from this place, and he would use Brady to find the man that had caused him to be sent here. If he did not find Reuben Latimer, and wring a truthful confession out of him that would clear O'Brien, O Brien would for the rest of his days be hunted by the law.

"That's right," O'Brien said. "I'm getting out of here. And I'm taking you with me. And we'll find Latimer together."

Brady rubbed his chin. "I'd take you to him," Brady said. "If we *could* get out of this stinkhole. But you might as well forget it, O'Brien. You saw what happened when a prisoner tried to steal a couple sticks of dynamite. He's dead and buried now, and look what happened to Brown just because he knew about it and kept quiet."

"Listen," O'Brien said urgently, "I want to know where the dynamite is hid."

Brady grimaced. "You're looking to get yourself killed. The slow way."

"Would it be as slow as this?" he said.

"No," Brady admitted with a hard sigh. "Not as slow as this."

"Then you and The Owl get to Brown," O'Brien said. "He may know."

"You think he'd say, after what he's been through?" Brady said.

"You tell him," O'Brien said slowly, "that if he don't tell, I'll kill him." O'Brien meant it.

Brady looked into his eyes. "Okay. We'll talk to him."

That same evening, after they had been fed in the cell, Purvis came to get O'Brien. With no explanation whatever, O'Brien's hands were tied and he was taken to the frame building that served as Steiner's dwelling, office and persuasion cell. O'Brien was taken to a room at the back of the place where Steiner sat behind an old desk and Quinn sat smoking a cigar on a straight chair. There were two guards besides Purvis. In the center of the room was a table with a man shackled to it.

"I brought you here to show you something," Steiner said to O'Brien after the door was closed.

O'Brien looked from Steiner's hard face to Quinn's, then his gaze returned to the pallid man on the table. The man moved against the shackles fearfully.

"Before I show you, though," Steiner said, "I want you to understand that we know about Reuben Latimer and your association with him. Also, that before we're through with you, you'll tell us where he is."

"I don't know where he is," O'Brien said.

Quinn made an ugly sound in his throat.

"This first visit here is a free one, O'Brien," Steiner said smoothly. "Just to show you how we operate. You won't be asked to tell about Latimer this time. You'll just watch our— interrogation of another prisoner. McAfee is his name. He was caught digging a tunnel. We know there must have been others in on it, but he won't tell us who they are."

"There are no others," the pale man on the table mumbled.

"All right," Steiner nodded to Quinn.

Quinn and a guard went to the table. The guard reached to a wall and took down a heavy pair of pliers. At a nod from Quinn, he applied the pliers to the man's nose.

"What are the names of your accomplices?" Quinn said.

"There— was no one else," McAfee said in terror.

The guard tightened the pliers and broke cartilege and bone in the man's nose. Blood spattered onto the guard's shirt front, and McAfee let out a yell, then lay there moaning.

O'Brien grimaced. He looked from the table over to the wall again, and saw the sharp instruments there, and the blunt instruments, and the tools with cutting edges. And he wondered what kind of men Steiner and Quinn were.

"What do you say now?" Quinn was saying to the victim.

But McAfee had no answers for them. So the guard went and got other tools. Teeth were broken off in the man's mouth, and then it got worse. They ripped flesh from the prisoner, broke more bone, and finally twisted off a couple of fingers. Anger was building in O'Brien as he tried to ignore the yelling. O'Brien was about ready to start calling Steiner names, when the man named McAfee passed out.

Quinn looked frustrated. "Want to try to bring him around?' he said to Steiner.

"No," Steiner said in a low voice. "Kill him."

O'Brien stared at Steiner. He must be insane. McAfee obviously had nothing to tell anybody. Quinn aimed a revolver at McAfee and blew the back of his head off. O'Brien looked over at Steiner as Steiner turned to him.

"Well, that's how it works, O'Brien," he said in a soft, smooth voice. "You can see that we have all the implements to get the job done. And we don't quit until we find the truth."

O'Brien just stared at him, and tried hard not to let the hatred show in his eyes.

Quinn was holstering his gun. He looked toward O'Brien as if he would like to start on him now.

"Now you go back to your cell and you think on what you just saw," Steiner told O'Brien. "And in a few days we'll bring you back here and see if you've had a change of heart. Of course, if you change your mind in the meantime, you just tell Purvis here."

O'Brien considered the warden gravely, and wondered whether he prefered that he talk, or not talk. He knew about Quinn for sure. "I'll keep that in mind," he said. "Mr. Steiner."

In the next couple of days, three men at the prison died of malnutrition or disease, and one was brutally beaten to death in the mine by a guard. General morale was very low. When Brady heard of O'Brien's session with Steiner and Quinn, he told O'Brien to go ahead and tell them that Latimer was in Villa Bella.

"I can't do that," O'Brien said. "It ain't right." But he had two very good reasons for not wanting to tell Steiner anything. If Castillo rode to Villa Bella after Latimer, he just might scare Latimer off without nailing him. And if he did get him, he might kill him without getting the truth from him about Sandy Creek, or force a false confession from him which would forever implicate O'Brien and brand him an outlaw.

"Do you want to go through what McAfee did?" Brady said.

"Not if I can avoid it," O'Brien told him. They were sitting in a back corner of the cage, and it was midnight and most of the other prisoners in the barracks were asleep. The Owl was huddled in another corner, twitching in a nightmare. "I'm still planning on a break-out. And, if you'll get on it, we'll make it before Steiner makes his next move."

Brady looked around them to see if anybody was listening. He turned back to O'Brien. "I waited till now to tell you, O'Brien. I found out today."

O'Brien looked over at him. "The dynamite?"

"That's right. I know where it's kept."

"Well?" O'Brien said.

Brady moved closer. "It's in the mine. In a side shaft near where we're working. When they blast, the guards go get some dynamite and hide it in the bottom of an ore car, wheel it up to the surface, then carry it back down like they got it from a supply building up here."

"That Steiner is a crafty bastard," O'Brien said.

"But there's no way you can sneak any out of there," Brady told him.

"We'll see," O'Brien said.

The next morning O'Brien worked hard in the mine. They were working their way down a shaft that had already been dug, widening the shaft, because the vein ran deep. They were very close to the side shaft that Brady had spoken of. O'Brien fixed the location of the shaft in his mind, and planned, and picked at the ore.

In late afternoon, O'Brien got the chance he was waiting for. He was within twenty feet of the side shaft, picking up ore and loading a car, when a prisoner down the line collapsed. The guard near O'Brien moved down to the man, and away from O'Brien, and began kicking and yelling at the prisoner. O'Brien hesitated only a moment, making sure the diversion would be a lengthy one, then turned and moved down to the side shaft and disappeared inside it.

He stood inside the darkness of the side shaft for a long moment, listening to the fallen man yell, and the guard's loud voice. Then he turned and groped his way back into the depths of the shaft. After moving along carefully for twenty yards, letting his eyes adjust to the almost total absence of light, O'Brien ran into the wooden chest on the floor. He felt it and there was a padlock on it.

O'Brien got down onto his knees and felt around and found a large rock near him. Turning back to the chest, he hammered at the lock viciously. After three hits, the lock broke, and he lifted the lid of the box. Inside was stacked, in row after row, the sticks of dynamite.

O'Brien grabbed at them, stacking a dozen of them in his arms, and then he quickly moved back to the mouth of the side shaft. He dropped the dynamite there, and looked outside. The thing between the guard and the prisoner was still continuing. O'Brien looked along the shaft and saw the brown cloth bag that the guard always carried down with him, which carried extra lanterns and pick heads and such. Two prisoners looked down toward O'Brien and he ducked back. When it looked clear, he came back out of the shaft, moved down to the bag, and picked it up. Brady, who had been working near him, now looked and saw O'Brien with the bag. O'Brien put his hand to his lips, and moved back to the side shaft. Inside its mouth, he dumped the equipment out of the sack, and filled it with the dynamite. Then he stepped back out with the sack. He had taken just a couple of steps, and the guard turned back toward him and saw him. The prisoners were hard at work.

"Hey, you!" the guard said. "What you doing down there?"

O'Brien saw that there were no other guards in sight. He held the bag in his left hand, and saw there was no use trying to hide it now.

"Something wrong down here, Boss," O'Brien said quickly. "I found your bag outside this shaft, and this man lying in here. He looks dead, Boss."

"What man?" the guard said. He moved cautiously down to O'Brien, stopping and looking at the bag O'Brien held before he moved on to the mouth of the side shaft.

When the guard pulled his gun and stepped to look inside the shaft, O'Brien swung the bag at the back of his head and there was a loud crunch and a gasp as the man fell forward into the shaft. O'Brien moved in after him, dropping the bag at the mouth.

When O'Brien moved into the darkness, the guard, dazed but conscious, turned and kicked at O'Brien's feet, knocking him down. Then the guard sought his dropped gun in the dark. O'Brien did not give him time to get to it, though. He threw himself onto the man, and smashed his fist into the side of his head. They struggled there on the floor of the shaft then, rolling around and slugging it out, and finally both were on their feet again.

"Guard!" the guard yelled.

O'Brien could not let him yell again. He lunged at the man, grabbing at his throat with his big hands, and closing them around the guard's neck. The man tried to yell again, but nothing came out. He pummeled O'Brien's head and body to get the big man off him, but then the beating became weaker, and O'Brien closed off the guard's air completely. The man went limp and O'Brien let him slump to the floor. O'Brien stood there breathing hard, remembering that he had almost died the same way at the hands of Short Hitch. He listened for running feet, but there were none. O'Brien went back to the entrance of the shaft, and looked out. Everything looked normal, and only Brady and a couple of other prisoners had seen the guard go into the shaft.

O'Brien picked the bag up and carried it down to where it had lain previously, and dropped it there. A couple of prisoners looked up, and then went back to work. They apparently had not heard O'Brien's story to the guard. Brady watched O'Brien return to work, and asked him with his eyes what had happened, but O'Brien just turned from him and picked at the vein of copper.

A short time later the work day was over. A couple of guards had come near O'Brien but did not ask about the guard. Just as the prisoners were moving out, however, a guard stopped near O'Brien and Brady.

"Where's Cramer?" he said.

He was refering to the guard O'Brien had killed, and who lay now inside the side shaft.

"He went back up early, Boss," O'Brien said. "But he left this." O'Brien handed the guard the closed brown bag.

The guard scowled at O'Brien. "Hmmph. Okay, I'll take it up. Now move your freight out of here."

"Right, Boss," O'Brien said.

Brady looked at O'Brien and moved on ahead of him toward the surface.

Up above later, O'Brien watched the guard move through the gate separating the two compounds, with the bag, and then O'Brien and Brady moved past the gate guard themselves, and were examined closely to see if they had brought anything out of the mine with them, a procedure which occurred every day. But there was nothing to find on O'Brien. The twelve sticks of dynamite were on their way to an equipment shed beyond the gate, in the prison compound. As O'Brien moved into that compound, O'Brien distinctly saw the guard move into the shed with two other guards, and dump the bag inside. Later, while O'Brien and Brady watched surreptitiously from a distance during their exercise period, they saw the shed locked with a heavy padlock, the dynamite inside.

"You mean it's in the bag?" Brady said to O'Brien, turning from the shed.

"That's it," O'Brien said.

Brady looked at O'Brien again, and shook his head slowly. "That's smart as hell," he said. "But where's that guard you lured into the side shaft?"

"Still in there," O'Brien said coolly.

Brady appraised O'Brien somberly. "You aren't kidding about all this, are you?"

"I ain't much for kidding," O'Brien told him. "Every guard I seen here deserves to be right down there with him. They're all loco mean, just like the men that picked them."

Brady grinned. "I like your style, O'Brien. But now that you've got a batch of dynamite in that shed, how are you going to use it to get us out of here?"

O'Brien rubbed a hand through his dirty, full beard. "I'm not quite sure yet," he said. "But it will have to be soon, whatever we do with it. When they find out about that guard, there will be trouble. Plenty of it. And a couple of prisoners saw me go in there with him. They won't keep quiet forever. Most of them would sell me out for a sack of tobacco."

"When you say 'soon', just how soon do you mean?" Brady said to the big man.

O'Brien glanced over at him. "Probably tonight," he said.

The guards did not miss their dead companion until the evening meal, and then there was no alarm about it. The man who had carried Cramer's cloth bag to the shed said that Cramer must have gone to speak with Quinn, in the warden's house, and volunteered to check there after eating.

In the meantime, the prisoners had been fed their one meal for the day, and darkness had fallen over the prison camp, and O'Brien was explaining his next move to Brady and The Owl, in their cell.

"They must have missed that guard by now," O'Brien said. "If we wait till Steiner and Quinn hear about what's happened, it will be too late. So you and me, Brady, are going to go get that dynamite, and use it."

"What are you going to do with it?" Brady said. "Blow the main gate?"

"To hell with the main gate," O'Brien said. "I'm planting this stuff under Steiner's office."

Brady looked at O'Brien and his lips formed a small smile. "You're going to try to get Steiner? That's great. But how's that going to get us out of here?"

"Think about it," O'Brien said. "That office is where Steiner has his weekly meetings with the guards, just about the time we go down into the mine. Well, I figure that when he hears about that guard, he'll call a special meeting, like he always does in an emergency or when there's trouble. He'll want to direct a look into it himself. Names of suspects, troublemakers, and so forth will be given to the guards. I figure there's a possibility the meeting might happen tonight, but more likely, tomorrow morning at the usual time. I'm going to try to catch them all in there."

Brady now really gave O'Brien a look, and his eyes narrowed on the big man. "You mean— get Steiner and Quinn and most of the guards in one blast?"

O'Brien regarded him with cold blue eyes. "Why not?"

Brady turned from O'Brien and stared blank-faced across the empty space of the cage. "Jesus!" he said.

"By God!" The Owl whispered harshly.

Brady looked back at O'Brien. "You— think there's really a chance to do that?"

"I'm *going* to do it," O'Brien said. "And you're going to help."

"Jesus, that would be something!" Brady said.

"Something a man could take to his grave with him."

O'Brien grunted. "Did you get that gadget before they herded us in here?"

Brady reached under his gray dungaree shirt and produced a wire device for picking locks, which he had obtained from another prisoner in the compound. The man had made it for Brady on short notice. "I had to tell some people what's going on," Brady said. "I hope they don't talk."

"We have to take that chance," O'Brien said. He looked at the gadget, which was small in his big hands. "This is supposed to do it?"

"Yes," Brady said. "It should also open the padlock on the equipment shed."

Just then the guard called Purvis walked through the place, looking into the cells and making his early evening check. O'Brien stuck the device into his trousers. Purvis eyed the three of them as he passed, and then moved out of the barracks at the other end.

"Now's as good a time as any," O'Brien told Brady, grabbing the lock pick once more. He fumbled with it. "Maybe you better work this."

He gave it to Brady, and Brady turned to the cage door. Prisoners down the line were alerted now to what was going on, and watched silently as Brady stuck the pick into the lock. He fiddled with it for several minutes, and then those within earshot heard the tumbler click as the device moved it.

"That did it!" Brady whispered harshly to O'Brien.

O'Brien moved to the door and pushed it open into the aisle, looking down toward the door for any sign of Purvis. Then O'Brien turned back and looked past Brady to The Owl. "If Purvis gets back before we do, tell him Quinn came and took us."

The Owl nodded. O'Brien and Brady moved into the aisleway and shut the cell door behind them. They were on their way.

Outside, the night was pitch black. Most of the guards were in the long mess building, except for the ones on the towers. O'Brien reached the equipment shed without incident, keeping in deep shadow as much as possible. Brady picked the lock quickly. O'Brien went inside and found the brown bag and the dynamite was still in it. He grabbed a length of fuse from a shelf, and re-joined Brady outside.

"Okay. Let's head for Steiner's quarters," he said in a whisper.

They moved to that building undetected. There was a guard on the front porch of the place, but he was busy twisting up a smoke and did not see them. They crouched beside the building, which was set off the ground on corner posts, its underside open to entry. When they were sure the guard was otherwise occupied, they crawled under the building on their bellies. Shortly, O'Brien was under the room Steiner used as an office. He and Brady unloaded the dynamite, listening to voices in the room above them, working silently.

"Maybe Cramer went into town," Steiner's voice came indistinctly. "But if he isn't here for breakfast, we'll have a little meeting here to discuss what action to take."

O'Brien and Brady exchanged glances. O'Brien hooked the fuse up, and then punched Brady and they began crawling back to the edge of the building, unrolling the fuse. When they got there, and were out from under the building, O'Brien cut the fuse.

"Now let's get out of here."

Brady reached into a pocket and produced a garotte, a strangulation instrument made of a length of wire with two handles. "A Cajun from New Orleans in barracks five gave it to me. In case we meet a guard."

O'Brien grunted and they moved out. They avoided the porch guard and got to the first barracks building without trouble. A tower guard looked toward them, but did not see them. Brady had just started out toward their own barracks, with O'Brien waiting behind him, when they both heard the voice from the barracks they had been hiding at.

"Hey, you!"

A guard who had just exited from the barracks had seen Brady. Brady turned toward him, trying to hide the garotte.

"What you doing out here?"

When the guard reached him, Brady panicked and struck at the guard with the garotte handles, using the weapon as a club. There was a scuffle and the garotte dropped to the ground. O'Brien came up behind them, picked up the garotte, and slipped it over the guard's head, pulling savagely on the wood handles. The wire cut through flesh, tendon and muscle, almost decapitating the guard. The guard hit the ground without an outcry. O'Brien looked at the blood spattered on him.

"Move," O'Brien said to Brady.

Brady stumbled into the shadows of their barracks while O'Brien rolled the body of the guard under the barracks where the fight had occurred. Then O'Brien joined Brady at their barracks and they went inside. A few moments later, they were back in their cell.

"It's planted," Brady said to the others.

O'Brien removed his dungaree shirt and turned it inside out so the blood would not show. Just then Purvis appeared in the doorway to the compound. O'Brien had the shirt back on.

"It sure is quiet in here tonight," Purvis said. "You boys planning a break or something?" He laughed loudly at his joke and turned and left the building.

The whole camp was awake early the next morning, in anticipation of the attempted break. Lock picks were fashioned and doors were silently unlocked. Each barracks was to be responsible for its own guard, but most of them were expected to be in Steiner's office when it happened.

Purvis came around early and announced that nobody was going into the mines until the morning meeting in Steiner's office was over. O'Brien stopped him before he left.

"Yeah, what is it?" Purvis said.

"I heard something about Cramer," O'Brien said.

"What is it?" Purvis asked slowly.

"I'll talk to Steiner," O'Brien said, pointedly.

Purvis thought that one over, then decided to take O'Brien to Steiner's office with him. He unlocked the cell door and O'Brien accompanied him outside. They crossed the compound together in the early sun and O'Brien stopped him again when they arrived beside the building housing the warden's quarters.

"I better tell you something before we go in there," O'Brien said.

O'Brien had stepped over beside the building, out of sight of the other guards who were approaching the building. As soon as Purvis moved up beside him, warily, O'Brien turned quickly and threw a big fist into Purvis' face. The blow broke Purvis' nose and threw him back against the building. O'Brien picked up his dropped club then, and struck Purvis across the head with it, and Purvis slid to the ground. O'Brien looked and saw a guard looking at him.

"Hey, what the hell!" the man said.

O'Brien ran to the place at the building where he knew the fuse was waiting. He lighted a match as he heard the running steps coming at him. He lighted the fuse, knowing that most of the guards were already inside now.

"What you doing there?" the guard yelled. He had pulled his revolver.

O'Brien saw the fuse burn out of sight under the building. Then he took one look at the guard, and ran for the nearest barracks building. The guard yelled again, and then fired at O'Brien, and the slug splintered the wood of the barracks as O'Brien reached it. O'Brien ducked around the corner of the building, and reached for the club he had stuck into his belt. The guard came running around the corner and O'Brien swung the club hard into his face. The gun went off again, hitting nothing, and the guard dropped onto his back, with a bloody face. O'Brien just had time to duck to the ground before the explosion.

There was an ear-splitting roar, and O'Brien could see the wood and debris, mixed with human forms, flying high into the air. Shards of wood came crashing against the barracks he was hiding behind, and then the debris came falling out of the sky. A man's leg fell heavily beside him on the ground, and he noted with a great deal of satisfaction that the leg wore Quinn's pants. The smoke was still rising skyward when he regained his feet, and the prisoners rolled out of the barracks buildings. Everybody just stood for a moment staring at the blasted remains of the building, including the guards in the towers and the few left on the ground, all of them realizing that Steiner and Quinn and most of their staff were dead. It was a frozen, unreal moment, a moment of suspended time, and then suddenly it was over and there was chaos.

The guards on the ground ran for cover and began firing at the rampaging prisoners. The guards in the towers swung the big Gatling guns into operation and began blasting into the compound. Men began falling all around O'Brien.

O'Brien reached for the guard's gun beside him, and fired at a guard nearby and killed him with one shot. Then, while Brady and a group of prisoners were ramming the door of the guards' barracks, after guns and ammunition, O'Brien made his way to the back corner of the compound, where there was a small stable and a wagon.

Bullets flew all around O'Brien, digging up the dirt at his feet, as he ran. He was running almost into the mouth of the gun on one of the rear towers, but the guard firing it had a lot of prisoners to fire at and did not concentrate on O'Brien. Just as he reached the stable, though, O'Brien was shot in the left leg and knocked to the ground.

O'Brien examined the wound and it was superficial. He regained his feet and moved into the open stable. Inside, he found a horse and unpicketed it and took it outside and hitched it to the doubletree of the wagon standing outside. Then he returned and got a second horse and hitched it up. He worked behind the cover of the stable. When he had the wagon ready, he climbed aboard and sized up the situation. Brady, according to plan, had broken into the guard barracks and had gotten guns for them. Then he had taken a couple of men to the gate, firing with rifles and revolvers as they went. One of the men with him had been killed, and another wounded in the stomach. Brady arrived unhurt and shot the lock off the gate and threw it open. The guards in the front towers were dead.

O'Brien whipped the team, and the wagon rolled down between the barracks and out into the open exercise area, toward the gate. The Gatlings from the rear towers turned toward him, but he was moving away from them now at high speed.

As O'Brien approached the gate, he saw The Owl struck by a bullet in the head, and thrown to the ground directly in front of O'Brien. O'Brien drove over the body and kept going. Five prisoners tried to jump on the wagon as it passed, while others were streaming from the gate on foot. Two of the five trying for the wagon made it, and then O'Brien roared through the gate, pulling Brady onto the wagon with his free hand as he went.

Another guard had mounted one of the front towers now, and directed the Gatling at the thundering wagon. The bullets tore up the wood of the wagon bed, and hit one of the two other prisoners in the thigh, but O'Brien and Brady were not hit. The wagon was out of range very quickly, when the guard then turned the gun on the running men on foot, and he mowed them down methodically, hitting the furthest from the gate first and working his way back. Then the other Gatlings concentrated on the gate, and no more men were able to leave through it. Within the next ten minutes, the prison break was put down by the remaining guards, with the surviving prisoners surrendering to the guns.

Sixty-three prisoners of the Bradenville prison had been killed or maimed by the guns on the towers, with the help of the guards on the ground. Twenty-seven guards had died, including the ones who had been caught in the warden's quarters when the explosion ripped that building apart. But Steiner and Quinn would not be around to count the losses.

Nine lonely, shocked guards shared the responsibility of getting the prisoners back into their cells. One hard-boiled old-timer went around and coldly shot each wounded prisoner through the head, and another one found a third horse, and rode off to Bradenville to get word to the state capital about the disaster.

O'Brien pulled the team up on the crest of a small sandy hill and looked back over the way they had come. Nobody was pursuing them. He had not thought there would be anyone, since so few were left at the prison.

Brady sat beside him on the seat, with a big grin on his face. "By God, you got us out of there," he said, still not believing it. "And we got Steiner and Quinn to boot. Now that's what I call a prison break."

The other two men were sitting in the wagon. They had tied a piece of cloth around the wounded man's leg. O'Brien was just letting his flesh wound clot on its own. He looked different from the way he had on that far-off morning when he had met the mule skinners on the trail. He had a full beard now, and was bare-headed, with his long hair wild, and wore the dirty gray dungarees. The only item from his original clothing was his boots. He thought of his gear now, and the appaloosa, and Castillo.

"Where are we headed?" Brady said to him. "If you want to go to Villa Bella, you have to turn south."

O'Brien looked south, and then back in the direction they had been heading. "Last Hope ain't far from here," he said. "I think I'll just pay Castillo a visit before we head south for the border."

"It's risky," Brady said.

"What ain't?" O'Brien said.

O'Brien was just about to start the team up, when he heard the voice behind them. "Hold it up right there," the command came.

It was the convict who was armed and unhurt. He pointed a guard's pistol at them now.

"What's the matter with you?" Brady said indignantly.

"Me and Ned here, we kind of took our own vote," the man said. His name was Williams and he had been in for murder in Ellsworth. "We're going south with the wagon, and you two is getting off here."

O'Brien looked hard at the man over his big shoulder, but said nothing. He had not wanted any passengers in the first place.

"You'd put us off?" Brady said loudly. "You wouldn't be outside the gate of that place if it wasn't for O'Brien."

"I'm much obliged for that," Williams said in a hard voice. "But now I'm heading south. And I don't need no excess baggage. Off." He motioned with the gun.

"He's got us shaded," O'Brien said to Brady,

shrugging his shoulders. He started to turn back to the horses.

"Just drop that gun first, O'Brien," Williams said.

"He's wearing it in his belt, in front," Ned said.

"Oh, sure," O'Brien said. He moved his hand toward the gun and kicked the left-side horse in the rump with his boot at the same time.

The horse jerked the wagon forward as O'Brien went for his gun. Williams was pulled off-balance by the motion of the wagon, and fell backwards, the pistol pointing skyward. O'Brien pulled the gun in his waist and fired twice at Williams. Williams took slugs in the low abdomen and middle chest, throwing him back onto Ned, who cowered away from him, eyeing O'Brien now wildly.

O'Brien aimed the gun now at Ned, and Ned gasped. "Don't!" he said.

"Kill him," Brady said angrily.

"Get off the wagon, and take your dead friend with you," O'Brien said, as Brady quieted the team.

"Sure," the other man said.

The man called Ned got off awkwardly with his bad leg, then laboriously pulled the body of Williams after him.

"Now you can head south just any time you feel like it," O'Brien told the man. Then he whipped the team and left the man standing there.

O'Brien went directly to the jail when he got to Last Hope, with the gun in his waist. He had not decided whether to just shoot Castillo, or merely make him wish he had. He was surprised to see the appaloosa standing outside the building. O'Brien's rifles were still on its irons, just as he had left them when he was arrested. He and Brady got off the wagon and a couple of men recognized O'Brien and hurried off in the opposite direction, fear written in their faces. As they walked to the entrance of the place, Brady pulled the gun he had taken from Williams.

"This is my show," O'Brien said to him.

"All right," Brady said.

When they entered the place, they found a man sitting on a hard chair, but he was not Castillo. It was one of the men who had brought O Brien in, and he was wearing a badge. When he saw O'Brien, his face crumpled in dismay.

"Where's Castillo?" O'Brien said.

"He's— out of town," the man stammered. "Be gone for several days."

O'Brien muttered a profanity, then looked back at the deputy. "You're one that brought me in, ain't you?"

The man swallowed hard. "I was one of them."

"And you're a regular deputy now?"

"That's right. Look, about your mount outside— Castillo said it was up for sale, and I—"

"Hell," O'Brien said, thinking of Castillo. He glared at the deputy, wanting to take his pent-up rage out on him. "Is there still ammunition for the rifles on the irons?" he said.

"Yeah, it's all there, just like you left it," the deputy said eagerly. "It's yours, if you want it."

O'Brien looked at him sourly. "That's real nice of you," he said. "Look, I want a mount for this fellow here, a good one."

"All right," the deputy said. He just wanted to

live through this. He did not care what O'Brien asked for.

"And get us both some clothes. I'll take a new set of rawhides, a big set. At the general store. And I want you to come up with that money you took from me. You can take the clothes out of the money."

"I ain't got that," the deputy said. "You'll have to ask Castillo about that."

"Well, then, you just get a loan from these nice merchants," O'Brien said, "and let Castillo pay them back. You be back with all that in an hour, or we'll come after you."

The deputy looked from O'Brien to Brady. "I can tell you he means it," Brady said.

"Yeah," the deputy said. "Okay. I'll be back."

"And if you cause us any trouble," O'Brien said, as the man went to leave.

"Yeah?" the deputy said.

"I'll kill you," O'Brien told him.

The deputy was back before the hour was up. The merchants had come up with the money and told the young man to cooperate. They did not want trouble, not with Castillo gone. Brady and O'Brien washed up at a well out in back of the place, and found a razor and cut the beards off, and when the deputy returned with the clean clothes and they put them on, they felt like different men. O'Brien donned the rawhides and a new Stetson, and he felt like a man again, rather than an animal. When he mounted the appaloosa, the stallion felt good under him. The deputy had taken good care of it.

He looked over at the deputy standing in the

doorway of the jail, then at Brady on the new mount. "Let's ride," he said.

Reuben Latimer sat drinking tequila at the table in the center of the room. Sarge was standing against a wall, massaging his shoulder. He had just taken his arm out of a sling, from the gunshot wound in the bank robbery. Waco sat across the table from Reuben, watching Reuben's face. Ayers and Sidewinder were in town, at the cantina.

"I think we'll go for the same place twice," Reuben said, taking a swig of tequila and then biting on a slice of lemon.

"The bank in Hodgenville?" Sarge asked incredulously.

"The same," Reuben said. "Next week we'll clean them out again."

Waco regarded Reuben somberly. He thought it was a lousy idea, just like Sarge, but he had learned quickly that Reuben was not a man you argued with, not unless you were prepared to challenge his leadership. And Waco was biding his time for that.

"You're crazy as a coot!" Sarge said loudly. He was already fed up with Reuben. He should have known when he deserted with him, he thought now, that the man was no leader. He was too thick-headed for leadership. And too ornery to follow somebody with more brains. It made a bad combination.

Reuben glowered at him. "Don't you ever say that to me," he growled at Sarge.

Sarge was in no mood to placate Reuben, though. "You go in there again, you'll get us all killed. They're riled up there. They'll be laying for us. I heard a federal marshal is looking into the last robbery. We got to bide our time, or hit somewhere else."

Reuben took the last swig of tequila from the glass and forgot the lemon. He wiped at his mouth with a big hand. "You'd like to run this outfit, wouldn't you, Sarge, old pal?" He had put an ugly grin on.

Sarge hesitated. "Hell, no," he said. "I just want to keep my skin."

"He doesn't mean anything, Reuben," Waco reasoned.

"Shut up," Reuben said.

Waco stared over at Reuben with slitted eyes. Waco was faster than Reuben, but he knew that he would have to fire several times to kill him. And by that time, Waco might have stopped some slugs himself. No, he would not challenge Reuben openly.

Reuben looked from Waco to Sarge. "If you think so goddam much of your skin, maybe we ought to leave you outside the next time, to watch the mounts."

Sarge's face darkened. "I ain't afraid to do what I have to," he said harshly. "But I got enough brains not to ride into a sure disaster."

"Oh, and I ain't got no brains, huh?" Reuben said. His face was flushed from anger and the alcohol.

"Oh, hell," Sarge said, trying to avoid a confrontation.

Reuben stood up from the table slowly, and faced Sarge. Sarge eyed him with a new look in his face. "You think a lot for a goddam coward," Reuben said in his low voice.

Sarge moved carefully away from the wall. His good hand moved out over his gun. He had taken all he could take from this low-grade moron, and he was not about to back away from him this time.

"You think a lot for a man that's got clabber for brains," Sarge said to Reuben.

Reuben was furious. "Well, let's see which counts now," he said to Sarge in a hard voice.

Reuben and Sarge went for their guns at the same moment. Waco had carefully moved aside, out of their line of fire. Sarge moved as quickly as he ever had, but he had never been as good as Reuben. Reuben fired first, hitting Sarge in the belly, and Sarge smacked up against the wall, dropping his gun. The explosion in the room shook the rawhide hanging over the windows. Sarge slumped against the wall, blood running through the fingers that held his stomach. Then Reuben fired again, hitting Sarge deliberately in the groin. Sarge yelled, and slid to the floor. Reuben let him lie there in pain for a long moment, a slight grin moving his mouth, then fired a third time, the slug tearing through Sarge's chest and destroying the heart. Sarge shivered once and was dead.

Reuben holstered his gun and poured himself another drink. "I don't know why I thought I needed him in the first place," he said more to himself than to Waco. He sat back down at the table, glancing at the corpse on the floor. "Now, let's talk about that bank job."

O'Brien and Brady sat at a table in the cantina and downed their drinks slowly. They had already asked about Reuben Latimer and found that he and his men frequented this place. So, Brady knew, he had been right in his guess that Reuben had come to his hideout here.

"Old Reuben will be surprised to see us," Brady said, grinning. He pushed his hat back and revealed his receding hair line. His wiry frame hunched over his drink, and his dark eyes looked into O'Brien's.

O'Brien sighed and sat back on his chair. "I got something to tell you, Brady," he said. Brady had recalled just where the hideout was, and told O'Brien roughly how to get to it, so O'Brien did not really need him anymore.

"Yes?" Brady said.

"I wasn't ever with Latimer."

Brady grinned for a moment, then when he saw the serious look in O'Brien's eyes, the grin slid away.

"You mean it," he said.

"It was pure accident that I rode up to that wagon on Sandy Creek right at that time," O'Brien said. "I told the sheriff right. I never heard of Reuben Latimer till the sheriff mentioned his name."

Brady narrowed his eyes on his new-found companion. "Then what are we doing here in Villa Bella?" he said.

O'Brien met his gaze. "I'm here to get Reuben Latimer," O Brien said. "And make him tell the law, if he lives, that I wasn't at the creek when the shooting took place."

"Then you just used me to—"

"I got you out of that rat's nest they call a prison," O'Brien reminded him.

Brady scowled at the big man, and then pounded

his fist on the table. "I'll be damned. I suppose it wouldn't occur to you to thank me, or apologize for bringing me here for nothing."

O'Brien shrugged. "I thought you might want to join me in bringing Reuben in."

Brady stared at him. "You're crazier than I thought, O'Brien, and that was crazy enough. You mean you're really going to try to take that bunch by yourself?"

"If I have to," O'Brien said.

"Well, count me out, buffalo man," Brady said. He swigged the rest of his drink. "I guess this is where our trails separate. I don't hold any grudges for bringing me here by pretext, but I'm not going after Reuben, either."

O'Brien laid his big hand on the Winchester rifle he had put on the table when they sat down. "You wouldn't ride out there ahead of me and warn him, would you?"

Brady held his gaze. "I don't make any promises to anybody," he said deliberately.

They sat there for a long moment. Then O'Brien moved his hand from the rifle. "I don't blame you. See you around."

Brady stood just as the door to the cantina swung open. "See you, O'Brien—"

He turned with O'Brien to see two men who had entered. They were lawmen from across the border, and one was Castillo. Brady glanced at O'Brien and knew this.

The lawmen had their guns out. "Reach for the rafters," Castillo said to them.

O'Brien kicked the table over as he grabbed for the rifle and dived at the floor. Castillo shot at him and the slug ripped past O'Brien's ear and dug into the floor. O'Brien hit the floor and rolled behind the table. The other lawman fired and beat Brady, and hit Brady in the chest, knocking Brady across the room and killing him before he hit the floor.

The glass of a big front window broke, and O'Brien saw a deputy outside, the one he had dealt with in Last Hope when they passed through. The man had a rifle, and was aiming at O'Brien from a good angle. O'Brien fired the Winchester first, and hit the deputy in the throat and severed his spine, throwing the deputy back into the street outside.

Castillo fired again at O'Brien, chipping a piece out of the table, and just missing O'Brien on its far side. The federal marshal with him had dived behind the bar as O'Brien swung the Winchester toward him. O'Brien fired and just missed the marshal as he moved behind the bar. The slug split the wood and ricocheted across the room.

Castillo, out in the open, started for another overturned table near the door, firing toward O'Brien's table as he went. Two slugs hit O'Brien's cover, and they were deflected by it. O'Brien turned his rifle from the bar and fired twice at the hated Castillo. The first slug hit the other window of the place, behind Castillo, and crashed through the glass harmlessly, and the second caught Castillo in the lower back. The impact spun Castillo around sharply and threw him through the broken window, making another loud crash of glass as he fell to the walk outside.

The marshal then leaned out from his cover and fired off a round from his revolver at O'Brien, but the shot missed both O'Brien and the table he was using as cover.

"Castillo?" the marshal called from the bar.

"I think he's dead," O'Brien said from the table. "Just like that deputy he brought with him." He waited a moment for that to make its effect on the marshal. "Unless you got somebody else out there, it's between you and me, now."

There was a silence, then finally the marshal spoke. "Why don't you give it up, O'Brien?"

O'Brien grunted. "And go back to Bradenville?" he said. "That's not much of a choice for a man that shouldn't have been put there in the first place."

"You're still saying you're innocent?" the marshal said. Three scared customers and the bartender, all of whom had dropped to the floor when the shooting started, were now slowly raising their heads.

"I wasn't at Sandy Creek with Latimer," O'Brien said.

"What about the prison break?" the marshal said. "What about all the other men you've killed since you were arrested? What about these two men?"

O'Brien made a sound in his throat. "It all sprung from Castillo's ambition," he said. "A man's got a right to fight back when the law punishes him unjustly."

There was another silence.

"What are you down here for, if not to join Latimer?" the marshal finally said.

"To make him confess to the massacre, and say that I wasn't there," O'Brien said.

The marshal behind the bar lowered his gun slowly. "Let's talk, O Brien," he said.

O'Brien kept the rifle pointed toward the bar. "Sure. Just come out of there with your gun holstered."

In a moment the tall marshal rose from behind the cantina bar. He wore a mustache like O'Brien's, but it was darker. His gray eyes were the color of granite. He stepped out from behind the bar, with his gun holstered. O'Brien rose slowly and nestled the rifle under his arm.

"Please, senors, no more shooting," the bartender was saying.

The other customers hurried out the door and looked at the two dead men lying in the long afternoon shadows, then moved off. O'Brien and the marshal stood where they had shown themselves, and conversed at that distance.

"You know where Latimer's hiding out?" the marshal said.

"I do," O'Brien told him.

"And you're going out there to get him?"

"I am."

"Hmmm." The federal marshal rubbed his chin, "You mind if I went with you?"

O'Brien regarded him for a long moment, his blue eyes appraising the other man studiedly. "If you'll leave Latimer to me," O'Brien said. "I want him alive."

"That's a deal," the marshal said. He walked over to O'Brien. He stood a couple of inches shorter than the buffalo hunter, and was not as broad. "The odds will still be two to one or worse."

"That's better than I expected," O'Brien said.

O'Brien and the marshal, whose name was Carter, left the cantina then, after the marshal arranged for burial of Brady, Castillo and the deputy, and they rode out to find the Latimer place together.

At the hideout, Reuben walked to the open front door of the adobe house and threw a washpan of dirty water onto the ground outside the door. He stood there then, his broad face staring out over the burnt sienna horizon where the sun was setting. It was a good, safe place he had picked out here, he thought. But after they hit the bank at Hodgenville again next week, they would be able to move north again, and hit deeper into Texas, now that the Sandy Creek thing had cooled down.

Ayers walked over to the door with an armload of kindling wood, taking it inside. "How's that Indian doing with the chow?" he said as he passed Reuben.

"It won't be long," Reuben said. He turned and followed Ayers in. "Hey, Maria, move your freight!"

A Mexican woman whom Reuben kept for bed and food was making tortillas over an open stove. Waco was looking at a map of Bradenville which he himself had drawn earlier, and Sidewinder was heckling the woman at the stove.

"Is that grub, or hog slop?" he grinned, standing near her.

Reuben closed the door behind him. Ayers went and lighted the lamps, and there was a cozy glow to the place. It was the closest thing to a home that Reuben had had since he was a kid. He kind of hated to leave the place for greener pastures, but money was what he wanted. Money and more money. A man could never get too much of it, no matter how he tried.

"*Algo mas, senora?*" Waco said when Maria set a plate of the tortillas on the table, asking if there was anything else.

Reuben glared at him. He did not like it that Waco used words in English he had never heard before, and could speak Spanish to Reuben's woman.

"*Disponemos de un gran surtido, senor,*" Maria said to Waco, telling him she had a large selection for the meal.

"Talk in Texas talk," Reuben said to them. He sat down at the table while Waco removed the map, avoiding Reuben's eyes. Sidewinder sidled up and seated himself opposite from Reuben, and then Ayers moved over and looked at the food.

"Jesus," Ayers said. "I can't eat this crap much longer."

"Sit down and shut up," Reuben told him.

Ayers stood there shaking hs head. "I still say that ain't real—" He paused. "Did you hear something?"

"One of the mounts," Waco said, taking a tortilla.

"Yeah," Ayers said suspiciously. "But it sounded like it come from the other side of the place."

"Your ears are playing tricks on you," Sidewinder said, biting into a tortilla crammed with a meat filling.

"Maybe, but—"

"Sit down!" Reuben said.

But then another sound came, and they all heard it. The three sitting at the table were frozen in their positions, with Ayers turned toward the door, standing, and Maria over by the stove, when it happened. The door that Reuben had recently closed suddenly burst open savagely, and two men blew into the room like buffalo in a stampede. It was O'Brien and the marshal.

"It's the law!" Ayers yelled.

O'Brien held the Winchester and the marshal had pulled his red-boned Remington revolver. When Ayers panicked and drew, dropping into a half-crouch, O'Brien fired and caught Ayers in the left arm. Ayers' gun went off into the ceiling of the place, and he was spun to the floor as Maria screamed loudly and huddled into a corner.

In the meantime, Reuben dived away from the table and Waco threw the table up onto its side, the food flying across the floor. Waco drew like lightning and knelt for cover as Sidewinder turned and tried to run for an adjoining room.

Waco's gun went off simultaneously with the marshal's revolver, and they both were hit. Waco's shot dug into the marshal's side, tearing a flesh wound there, and the marshal's, because he did not have to draw, hit its mark and slammed into Waco's gun arm, flinging Waco's gun across the room.

O'Brien whirled and found Sidewinder as he neared the door leading from the room, and pulled off two shots to stop him. They hit Sidewinder in the shoulder and side, and the latter shot killed him, catapulting him into the other room, where he died almost immediately.

Reuben had pulled his gun from his position on the floor, and started to aim it at O'Brien when

O'Brien whirled on him with his rifle. Reuben saw the big muzzle pointed at his head, and lowered the gun.

"Drop it!" O'Brien said loudly.

Reuben reluctantly dropped the revolver to the floor. Maria was still screaming from a corner. The marshal turned his gun on Ayers and Ayers knew he was beat, too. "You, too," the marshal advised him.

Ayers glared at the marshal. "I'll get you for this," he said in his taut, low voice.

"Where you're headed, you won't be getting anybody," the marshal said, meaning the gallows.

Waco stood slowly and looked at the two men who had taken them. He had built a big respect for the one with the rifle, and was surprised that he was dressed like a hunter. He fought like a professional gunfighter, Waco thought.

Slowly, one at a time, they were on their feet. Ayers watched the lawman carefully, like a trapped rat. Reuben, angry at first that they had let this happen to them, now had regained his composure.

"You must be the hunter," Reuben said to O'Brien.

"That's right," O'Brien said. The woman had quieted down. O'Brien walked over to Reuben while the marshal kept Ayers and Waco under his gun.

O'Brien swung the rifle around and caught Reuben hard alongside the head, and knocked him down again. Reuben hit the floor hard, then sat there stunned, looking at O'Brien, his head bleeding. He focused on the big man and cursed him.

"Goddam you—" he said thickly.

"Who was with you at Sandy Creek?" O'Brien said.

Reuben glared at him. "None of your goddam business."

O'Brien aimed the rifle at his head. "Who was with you at Sandy Creek?"

Reuben grunted. "That marshal there ain't going to let you kill me. He wants to hang me too bad."

O'Brien fired the rifle and tore part of Reuben's left ear off. The barrel was so close that he could not hear for a moment, and there was a powder burn on his cheek. He jumped and grabbed at the bloody ear. Breathing heavily now, he looked back up at O'Brien with a different look on his face.

"He'll kill me, marshal!" Reuben said loudly.

"Who was with you?" O'Brien said. He cocked the rifle. "I already went through hell in your place. And my patience is thin."

Reuben grimaced and held the ear. "All right. It was Ayers there—"

"Don't tell him nothing!" Ayers yelled.

"—And a man called Sarge. The other one is dead."

"Anybody else?" O'Brien said. He kicked Reuben viciously in the thigh. "Anybody else there?"

Reuben grunted in pain. "All right, you wasn't there," he said in a low voice.

The marshal glanced over at him. "You absolutely sure about that?" he said.

Reuben looked up at the buffalo hunter. "Hell, yes, I'm sure. Nobody but a fool like Castillo would have thought so in the first place."

O'Brien lowered the rifle, and turned to the marshal. The marshal looked at him and then at Reuben. "Well," he said.

10

Marshal Carter and O'Brien took Reuben Latimer and his two remaining men to San Antonio which was the marshal's headquarters. There they were thrown into jail and their wounds tended, to await a detachment from Fort Custer, where Reuben and Ayers deserted. The army would try Reuben and Ayers, and a federal judge in San Antonio would decide Waco's fate. If any of them were freed on the charges that would be brought in those respective tribunals, there were fugitive warrants on them from other states. As for O'Brien, the marshal asked him not to leave town for a few days, and beyond that he was tight-lipped. O'Brien, wanting the matter to be decided once and for all so he could get back to hunting, obliged Carter and got a room at one of San Antonio's more modest hotels. On his second afternoon in town, he was sitting in the Stage Trail Saloon alone, thinking about all that had happened to him in the last month or so, when the marshal found him there. The tall, mustached Carter came to O'Brien's table with a small grin on his face.

"I just sent a telegram to the governor," he said, after O'Brien had nodded to him. "I mentioned you in it."

"Sit down," O'Brien said.

"Can't. I'm on my way somewhere. But I wanted to find you and tell you I'm asking the governor for a full pardon for you."

O'Brien's eyes narrowed. "You mean it?"

"It won't be easy for him, after what happened at Bradenville. But he's been after Steiner for a long time himself. Just couldn't get any evidence against him. I think he'll pardon you. He owes me a favor."

O Brien looked up at him. "I'm much obliged, marshal. You just saved me from turning outlaw, I reckon."

"Then I did myself a favor," Carter grinned. "I wouldn't relish the notion of going out after you."

O'Brien returned the grin. "You're all right, marshal."

"Just stick around these parts until I get all this straightened out," the marshal said. "See you soon, O'Brien."

O'Brien nodded, and the marshal left the saloon.

That evening the marshal rode out of town on business, leaving his two deputies in charge at the jail. And it was about that time that Reuben decided he was not going to stick around for a hanging. He discussed escape quietly with Ayers and Waco in adjoining cells, and when one of the deputies left for the evening meal, Latimer decided to put their escape plan into operation. Ayers began moaning in his cell.

The deputy on duty glanced at him, but did not move. Ayers yelled loudly, and the deputy rose slowly from his chair.

"What the hell's going on in there?" he said.

He went and unlocked Ayers cell and warily approached Ayers, who was doubled over on his cot, holding his stomach. "What is it?"

Ayers glanced up with his face twisted up. "My side. It must be my appendix or something. Look, ain't it swollen there?"

The deputy moved around with his back to the bars separating Ayers' cell from Reuben's, putting himself just across the bars from Reuben. Reuben could not quite reach him. Suddenly Ayers rose and kicked out at the deputy, knocking him up against the bars. He then threw himself at the deputy, but the deputy swung and knocked him to the floor. When the deputy straightened from the encounter, he moved against the bars again.

Reuben's big hand came through the bars and clamped around the deputy's neck, pulling the man hard against the bars. Reuben reached for the deputy's gun, but could not reach it. The deputy was struggling to free himself desperately. Ayers was still on the floor, out of the action. Reuben had to act fast. He grabbed at the deputy's key ring, and tore it off the deputy's belt. The deputy was almost free of Reuben's grasp. Reuben got the big key to the cells and turned it in his hand and jammed it hard into and through the deputy's wide open left eye.

The weapon popped the eyeball, spattering wetness, and drove through it to smash bone and penetrate the brain behind. The deputy yelled out, then slid to the floor, his limbs jerking spasmodically, like a chicken with its neck wrung.

Reuben pulled the bloody key and ring through the bars. "Let's get out of here," he said in a low, hard voice.

Reuben unlocked their cells and they stormed out of the cellblock.

"Arm yourselves!" Reuben shouted.

He and Waco found revolvers, and Ayers took a Winchester rifle. Just as they were leaving the building, they ran head-on into the other deputy, who was returning from his evening meal.

Reuben recovered before the deputy, and drew and blasted a neat blue hole in the deputy's face. The deputy did a somersault and hit the ground dead.

A short time later, when O'Brien was having a slug of whisky before going for his supper down the street, a man ran into the saloon with his face flushed and eyes wide.

"They're gone!" he said loudly. "Both deputies is dead! It's awful down there!"

O'Brien stared hard at him. "Latimer? Latimer is gone?"

"I was there, mister," the man said breathlessly. "I saw the empty cells. And them bloody bodies. One of them—"

"Did they ride out?" O'Brien asked.

"That's right. That fellow over there said he saw them go." He pointed to a rough-looking drifter who had just walked in the door.

O'Brien turned from him and just stood there a long moment, letting it sink in. He could not just let Latimer ride off now. Not after all O'Brien had been through because of him. Not after Bradenville. And there was no time to wait for the marshal. No, it was clear that it was up to O'Brien now. Maybe it always had been.

O'Brien walked over to the drifter at the bar, with all eyes in the place on him. The man watched him approach with a hard look.

"Which way did Latimer ride out of here?" O'Brien said.

The drifter grunted and took a long swig of whisky and set the glass down. "I don't see how that's any of your business." He was a big man, with red splotches of eczema on his hands and face. He wore a bone-handled Colt revolver on his hip.

O'Brien's voice dropped in volume. "I won't ask you again."

The drifter laughed. "You ain't threatening me, are you, buffalo man?"

When the drifter saw O'Brien's face harden, he went for the Colt, but it never cleared the holster. O'Brien smashed a big fist into the man's face, breaking his nose in three places, and the drifter banged up against the bar so hard that he cracked a rib in his back. He rose slowly to his feet, dazed, crimson running from his nose, shock in his eyes.

"Which way did Latimer ride out?" O'Brien said.

The drifter went for the gun again. But O'Brien caught the gunhand as it pulled the iron clear, and twisted the wrist sharply. Bone snapped again and the man yelled. O'Brien drove a fist into the drifter's gut then, mashing the man's insides. The drifter's eyes squinted shut hard, and his breath came whooshing out as he bent double, grabbing at his belly. He staggered in a small circle then, and when he faced O'Brien again, O'Brien caught him a last time alongside the head as the drifter turned, lifting the man off his feet and depositing him in a heap on the barroom floor.

"Hot damn!" a man said from across the room.

"By Jesus!"

O'Brien leaned over the drifter, and pulled his head off the floor by the hair. "Which way?" he said in the low voice. "Which way did they ride?"

"South," the drifter mumbled through a bloody mouth. "They took— the trail south."

O'Brien stood tall over him. "You see?" he said to the man on the floor. "Underneath all that ugliness, you ain't such a bad fellow after all."

He turned then and strode out of the saloon. On his way to the door, a man who had laughed earlier, when the drifter had refused to answer O'Brien, now got in his way momentarily. O'Brien shoved him with one hand as he passed, knocking the man across a table, where he crashed to the floor, wide-eyed.

Then O'Brien was gone.

11

Reuben had in truth ridden south. Not to cross over to Villa Bella again, that place was unsafe. He holed up in a tiny crossroads border town in Texas, called Purgatory. It was just a trail junction with scattered false-front clapboard buildings and a cantina and wide dirt streets where the wind whipped the dirt into dust devils that clogged a man's eyes and mouth.

The three outlaws took over the saloon, where Latimer knew the proprietor, and spent the afternoon of their arrival drinking rot-gut whisky and tequila. Reuben was saying how he hoped his trail crossed O'Brien's again. "I'll break that man up good. I'll make chopped meat of him, by God. I'll cut his innards out and feed them to the hogs."

His tirade was cut short by the arrival of a short, swarthy man in the cantina. He approached the table of the outlaws with a nervous manner, holding a straw hat in his hands. "Gentlemen," he said.

Reuben regarded him with contempt. "You got something on your mind?"

Waco grunted a small laugh at the fellow's nervousness. Ayers just sat there studying his face darkly.

"I am from the people here," the short man began. "We have formed a committee. They sent me to speak with you."

"What the hell is he talking about?" Ayers said.

"Speak up, damn it," Reuben said.

"The committee," the little man continued, "wonders— how long you fine gentlemen will be here in Purgatory."

"I think he's trying to tell us something," Waco grinned.

"The committee wishes no trouble— in our town. They wonder if it would be convenient for you gentlemen to— limit your visit here— to perhaps forty-eight hours?" He did not dare raise his eyes to them.

"Get to hell out of here!" the bartender called out.

"No, wait," Reuben said slowly. "This man wants an answer to take back to his committee. Isn't that right?"

The small man nodded slightly.

Reuben rose from his chair and grabbed the small man by his shirt front and pulled him close to him. "Well, take this answer back to them for us," he said grimly. He grabbed the fellow with both hands and threw him across the room, and the man crashed over a table and chairs before he hit the floor hard. When he managed to struggle to his feet, Reuben was waiting for him.

Reuben grabbed him again and threw him against the bar and the small man's head cracked against the rail, dazing him so that he could not get up again. Then Ayers moved over to him. "Add this to the message," he said. He kicked the supine figure hard in the groin and an agonized yell came from the small man. Ayers watched him try to crawl away, then broke a chair over his back. Finally he kicked him in the face, and the small man passed out, his face bloody.

Reuben glanced at him from the table, after pouring himself another drink. "It does something for the force in a man's veins, to get a little exercise," he said.

Waco sat and looked and said nothing. He would not have done it that way, but Reuben would make his point to the committee. The message was that Reuben would be here until he wanted to leave, and that while he was here, the town was his.

"Who is he?" Reuben said to the bartender.

"He runs the general store," the bartender said.

"Ayers, take him down there and dump him in front of his place," Reuben told him. "They'll find him there."

Ayers grinned. "Okay. I needed to kick the riding kinks out of my legs, anyway."

O'Brien reined up at the edge of the small, bleached town. The sun was boiling overhead, and a hot dusty wind was moving down the wide street. Reuben Latimer's trail had led here, to this off-trail place, but O'Brien wondered whether he would still be here. He lifted his Stetson, wiped at the sweat on his brow, and replaced the hat. Then he drew the Winchester rifle from its saddle scabbard, and checked it for ammunition. Yes, he was set. He dug his big spurs into the gray appaloosa's sides, and moved into town.

When he got just a little way along the dusty steet, O'Brien saw Ayers. Ayers had just dragged the store owner to his place and was turning to head back to the saloon. A few frightened citizens watched from doorways. Ayers had taken his rifle from its carbine boot, and had it slung under his arm now. He turned toward O'Brien just as O'Brien was dismounting from the stallion.

Ayers squinted down the street across the fifty yards that separated them, and focused on the buffalo hunter. O'Brien stepped out into the middle of the street, recognizing Ayers immediately.

"Well, well!" Ayers said softly. He took a firmer grip on the rifle under his arm. He thought quickly of Reuben and Waco in the saloon, but they were too far down the street to hear if he yelled. Anyway, this was better. The hunter was carrying a rifle, too, and Ayers was the man to show him how to use one.

O'Brien knew now that Reuben was here, and that this would be where it would all happen. Either Reuben Latimer or O'Brien would not leave this town alive. There would be no confessionals this time. O'Brien was not in the mood for them. But first, he had to deal with Ayers.

The two riflemen moved a few paces closer to each other, each watching the other man's face. It was the eyes you had to watch, not the hands or anything else. You had to tell from the eyes. They stopped about forty yards apart, a long distance for pistols, but close up with the long guns. It became quite clear to O'Brien that Ayers was going to challenge him with the rifle.

"You run into people in the craziest places," Ayers said to O'Brien, making a small joke. He was confident and assured. He was very good with a rifle.

"Where are your friends?" O'Brien said.

"They're here. Down at the saloon. But you don't have to worry about that, because you ain't getting that far."

O'Brien took a couple more steps toward Ayers, his spurs tinkling in the hot breeze. The sun was a flat-iron on his neck. He looked down toward the saloon. He would rather have found them all together. "You aiming to stop me?" he said.

"I ain't aiming to do nothing," Ayers said. "I'm doing it." He had slid his hand onto the trigger assembly, as had O'Brien. The rifles were still pointing toward the ground.

"You sound pretty sure," O'Brien said.

"Oh, I am," Ayers told him. "You see, I got a whole box of army medals for shooting this thing." He grinned. "I don't like to brag, but I can put a hole in a silver dollar at fifty yards. With a crosswind."

O'Brien for once in his life did not mind the other man's running off at the mouth. He was calculating what he would do when he got past Ayers.

"You ain't got much practice with that one there lately, have you?" Ayers continued, playing cat and mouse and enjoying it. "I mean in prison and all."

O'Brien's eyes narrowed on Ayers. He did not like to be baited. And the mention of Bradenville brought back a hundred unpleasant memories. The rats and starvation and disease and the hot box and Steiner's little torture chamber. O'Brien remembered and became angry inside.

"Well, you should have kept up on your shooting, hunter. Because now, you're going to need it." Ayers moved his feet slightly apart, getting ready to make his move.

"You talk a nice shoot-out," O'Brien said in his low growl. "Now let's see if you got any guts to back up the talk."

He had struck a sore spot with Ayers. Ayers did not like to have his courage insulted. A gust of hot wind breathed across his hate-filled face, fanning his emotions higher, and then he made his move.

O'Brien saw the subtle change in his eyes before Ayers' hand started the rifle up. O'Brien flashed the Winchester into play, while Ayers' rifle was still coming up. O'Brien fired without aiming, twice in rapid succession, with the snick of re-cocking sandwiched between the double roar of the rifle. The first shot of O'Brien's smashed into Ayers' right thigh and fractured the bone in it. The hit threw Ayers' aim off slightly, and when his rifle went off, between O'Brien's first and second shots, the slug just grazed O'Brien's left arm. Then O'Brien's second shot tore into Ayers' chest just below the heart, staggering Ayers backward in the dust, his feet trying unsuccessfully to keep under his plummeting body. He hit the ground hard, but incredibly managed to hang onto the rifle. As the gunsmoke cleared, O'Brien lowered the Winchester and moved toward Ayers. Ayers, with the last of his strength, lifted the rifle and aimed it at O'Brien's chest.

O'Brien saw the move as the rifle came up. He swung the Winchester up again, dropping to one knee. Ayers' rifle and O'Brien's went off almost simultaneously. Ayers' shot whistled past O'Brien's head, and O'Brien's slug entered Ayers' forehead, just between the eyes. Ayers hit the ground flat, gap-mouthed, his life-blood running into the dust, clotting it.

O'Brien glanced at the saloon, and then moved quickly off the street, between two buildings on the same side of the street with the saloon, where he would be hidden from view from the saloon.

Inside the Spanish-style building, Reuben and Waco looked toward the street. They had heard the first shots, but had paid little attention to them. Now, they began to wonder whether Ayers had gotten into trouble.

"You want to see what's going on out there?" Reuben said casually, looking toward the bartender.

"Sure."

The bartender walked to the double swinging doors and glanced down the street. Then he moved through them for another look. He turned back to Reuben. "You better come out here," he said.

Reuben and Waco exchanged glances, and then both rose and walked to the doors and moved through them. When they saw Ayers' bloody corpse in the street, there was shock and surprise in their eyes. They both drew their guns, searching the empty street with their eyes.

"It's the law!" Reuben said, cursing then under his breath.

Waco was looking down toward the gray appaloosa stallion. "No, it isn't," he said in a grim voice. "It's O'Brien. There's his mount."

Reuben looked hard at the horse. "I'll be damned," he said. His eyes flicked over the rooftops across the street.

"He's probably alone," Waco said, but his voice did not show that he felt that that was any great cause for celebration.

"Yeah," Reuben said slowly. "Come on, let's get back inside."

Reuben paced the floor when the three of them were in the saloon again. He walked back and forth through a bar of sunlight that hung from a skylight in the roof. "We better go after him," he said.

Waco was checking his revolver, and massaging his gun arm. "What for?" he said. "I think if we stay put, he'll come here after us. That's obviously why he rode in here."

Reuben glanced at Waco. He hated it that Waco always had such damned bright ideas. But he was right. If they stayed put, the hunter would have to make his play. He had nobody to help him. Not in this town. Reuben grunted.

"All right, we'll stay here." He turned to the bartender. "Get that shotgun ready and stay behind the bar. When the hunter busts in here, use it on him. Blow him in half if you can. Waco, you set there at that table just like you didn't know nothing was going on. I want him to see you when he first comes in. You'll have your gun on him from up front, where he won't see me when he comes through the doors. I'll gun him from the side or back."

Waco let a small grin move his mouth. Reuben had put him in the most dangerous spot, and Waco could tell from Reuben's eyes that he welcomed an argument on it. But Waco did not mind his assignment.

"All right," Waco said. "If he challenges us from the street, we'll all fire from the windows and doors, right?"

"Right," Reuben said, moving to the corner. He looked through the window as he passed it, and there was no sign of life out there. "I can see the back door of the room from here, too. In case he tries something sneaky." He pulled his gun. "Listen, if he ain't killed by the first blast of gunfire— I want him."

Waco did not answer. He had no intention of playing games for Reuben. O'Brien was a man you killed. You didn't play with him. Waco had seen enough to know that. No, he would kill O'Brien dead, wounded or not. And then he would kill him again.

Outside, in back of the place, O'Brien was examining the roof line. He thought of busting in through the rear door, but they would probably be prepared for that, and he could not get both of them at once. This type of place often had a skylight, though, he knew, and if so, he might just give them a surprise. He removed his spurs quietly, then clambered onto a wagon beside the place, the rifle in hand. From there he stepped onto a shed roof, and then moved up to the main roof from there.

Inside the place, Reuben moved again to the window and looked into the street. "Why don't he come?" he said under his breath. He glanced at Waco, realizing that he was the only one of his men left now. Ayers, lying with a hole in his head in the street out there, had been the first man Reuben had approached when Reuben decided to desert the cavalry. And now he, too, was gone.

"Have patience," Waco said to him. "From what we've seen of him, the hunter is the kind of man that will come to us."

"Patience, hell," Reuben said, his hand gripping the gun hard. "I should have did what I wanted to. Went out and found him."

Waco watched the sunlight through the door. "You might be dead now if you had," he said.

Reuben turned a burning look at him, and returned to the table in the corner. The bartender took a better grip on the shotgun, which was sweat-slippery in his hands. He was getting nervous. "He ain't coming," he said.

"I think you're right," Reuben said, shooting a hard look at Waco. "If something don't happen—"

There was a sudden and loud crashing of glass above their heads. The bartender and Reuben got a glimpse of the plummeting form as it came, but not in time to react before it was in the room with them. It was O'Brien, leaping from the skylight onto the shoulders and back of the unsuspecting Waco as he sat watching the door.

Waco, unlike Reuben and the bartender, did not have time to see what was happening to him. O'Brien hit him like a meteorite, amid a showering of glass fragments. Waco was knocked off the chair violently, and thrown to the floor after cracking through the table. O'Brien had caught him with his feet, but a glancing blow. Waco suffered an immediate shoulder separation, dislocated neck vertebra, and a broken left arm. He hit the floor with a crash that merged with O'Brien's own.

As soon as O'Brien hit, the bartender aimed the big shotgun and boomed off a round. O'Brien had fallen forward when he hit, and the mass of buckshot tore a foot-wide hole in the thick wood floor, where he had landed a split-second before.

O'Brien fell onto his left side, twisted around by digging his boots hard against the wood of the floor, and raised the Winchester from the hip. He fired the long gun and it exploded loudly in the room, making a much sharper noise than the dull boom of the shotgun, and the slug tore through the bartender's upper chest, throwing him back against the shelves behind the bar, crashing more glass. He grunted loudly and hung there a moment, not slipping to the floor, then started bringing the shotgun down toward O'Brien again. O'Brien fired again, hitting the barman under the chin and making a blue hole there. The man slumped open-mouthed from sight, as the shotgun shook the place again, blasting through a front window.

Then O'Brien heard Reuben's gun as he thumbed the hammer back. O'Brien turned but it was too late. Reuben's first shot went off and caught O'Brien in the left shoulder. It spun him onto his side, and Reuben's second shot rang out and splintered wood beside O'Brien's head. O'Brien rolled with the spin, and came up into a sitting position as Reuben took careful aim at him a third time from the corner.

"Now, damn you!" Reuben said.

But O'Brien had brought the rifle into play again. He fired and cocked and fired in lightning movements despite the wound. The first time he hit Reuben in the right hip, fracturing it before the bullet ripped on through his lower abdomen. Reuben yelled loudly and grabbed at himself, crashing back into two chairs. But he caught the second slug too, this one hitting him under the left arm and slashing through both lungs and collapsing them before it left through a wide hole in his back.

Reuben's thick face stretched out of shape in all directions as he was flung backwards again, crunching and banging against the wall. He slid slowly to the floor, coughing up blood.

Another shot rang out then, and a slug sung past O'Brien's ear. Waco had raised onto one elbow and had weakly attempted to kill O'Brien with one shot to the head. But he was in no shape for accuracy, after being broken up so badly when O'Brien crashed down onto him. O'Brien cocked and fired again now, coming to one knee, and hit Waco in the low ribs. Waco gasped out a yell and fell back to the floor. He lay there trying to move his legs for a moment, then quit. His breath stopped with his eyes staring widely at the skylight through which O'Brien had leapt upon him.

O'Brien rose slowly and painfully to his feet. He examined his shoulder. Blood ran down his arm under the rawhides. He would have to get some medical help somewhere. He walked over past the wide-staring Waco to Reuben Latimer, looked at Reuben for a long moment, and grunted in satisfaction.

"That don't make us even for Bradenville," he said to the corpse, "but it helps."

When O'Brien went outside, there were some citizens of Purgatory out there and somebody had brought his mount up. They all just watched him silently, grateful and yet afraid. Then a girl walked up to him from the group of onlookers. She was a rather pretty girl, with dark hair, and she looked very much like the girl at Sandy Creek must have, before Reuben Latimer got hold of her.

"Will you come to my father's place?" she said to O'Brien. "He can dig that bullet out for you. And he's got a bottle of brandy just waiting for a special occasion."

O'Brien looked down at the girl, and he knew he would be able to put Bradenville and Sandy Creek and all the rest behind him now. "I think I'd like that, miss," the big man said.

SUNDANCE #40: THE HUNTERS

By Peter McCurtin

PRICE: $1.95 LB1010
CATEGORY: Western

SURVIVAL OF THE FITTEST

Manning, an English big-game hunter, hires Sundance to act as his guide hunting grizzlies in the mountains. What Manning really wants to do is hunt Sundance —a man-hunt, with the fittest surviving.

#1: BRAND OF THE DAMNED
BRONC

SUNDANCE #38: DRUMFIRE

By Peter McCurtin

PRICE: $1.95 LB976
CATEGORY: Western

SUNDANCE AND GERONIMO!

Apache chief Geronimo was released from a Florida prison camp on the condition that he must become a farmer in Oklahoma. It was up to Sundance to get the hated chief there alive. Their journey was destined for blood.

THE KANSAN #6: LONG, HARD RIDE

By Robert E. Mills

PRICE: $2.25 LB989
CATEGORY: Adult Western

EAGER WOMEN AND KILLING MEN

The Kansan's long chase begins when he learns that Deanna has left with the ruthless and deadly John Hartung. After a powdersmoke hell on the St. Louis docks, the Kansan continues his hard trail to New Orleans, where he finds the pleasure of old flames and the pain of hot lead!